'What made y

'I didn't realise it w

Each broke off to gesture for the other to continue.

'I was only going to say that I didn't realise it was *you* I was going to be working with,' Jack said.

'How could you *not* have known?' Lauren exclaimed in surprise.

'How was I supposed to know that Dr Scott-Dakers was once called Lauren Hamilton?' Jack pointed out with maddening logic. 'The last I heard you'd thrown in the towel at the hospital and gone back to live with Mummy and Daddy.'

There was just enough truth in his words to prevent her denying them.

Josie Metcalfe lives in Cornwall now with her long-suffering husband, four children and two horses, but, as an army brat frequently on the move, books became the only friends who came with her wherever she went. Now that she writes them herself she is making new friends, and hates saying goodbye at the end of a book—but there are always more characters in her head clamouring for attention until she can't wait to tell their stories.

Recent titles by the same author:

INSTANT FATHER CHRISTMAS
PROMISES TO KEEP
A LITTLE BIT OF MAGIC

BE MY MUMMY

BY
JOSIE METCALFE

MILLS & BOON®

All the characters in this book have no existence outside the imagination of the author, and have no relation whatsoever to anyone bearing the same name or names. They are not even distantly inspired by any individual known or unknown to the author, and all the incidents are pure invention.

First published in Great Britain 1999
Harlequin Mills & Boon Limited,
Eton House, 18-24 Paradise Road, Richmond, Surrey TW9 1SR

© Josie Metcalfe 1999

ISBN 0 263 81515 3

Set in Times Roman 11 on 12 pt.
03-9903-50119-D

Printed and bound in Norway
by AIT Trondheim AS, Trondheim

CHAPTER ONE

'HEY, Lauren, what happened at the meeting? Have they made any decisions about Holly yet?'

Sunila's anxious voice was the first thing Lauren heard over the usual hubbub of the ward, the perfect crescents of her friend's dark eyebrows drawn into a worried frown.

Lauren drew a deep breath and ran her fingers absently through the escaping strands of chestnut hair to tidy them away into the clip at the back of her head.

She'd hardly had time to set foot inside the door when Sunila had spoken, and her thoughts were lagging some way behind. The meeting she'd just attended had gone on longer than usual without a coffee-break, and it almost looked as if Sunila had been pacing the floor while she waited to pounce.

For St Augustine's hospital it had just been the usual weekly departmental meeting at which all the interested parties had discussed the various aspects of their patients' progress.

Today the small room had been full to capacity with the familiar gathering of doctors, registrars and so on. In keeping with her relatively junior status, Lauren had seated herself on a seat towards the corner nearest the door, ready to slip out if necessary. It had, however, given her a good vantage point from which to observe everyone else.

After baby Michael's death earlier in the week Lauren had expected to see Eric Alcala, the pathologist, in attendance with his sheaf of notes at the ready. She'd watched for a moment while he'd spoken to her immediate boss, Noah Kincaid, not needing to be able to hear the conversation between paediatrician and pathologist to know that they were both upset that the youngster hadn't survived.

Her eyes continued to make their circuit of the dozen or so people in the room.

Although she hadn't had time to get one for herself, she wasn't surprised to note that nearly half of the people there had brought a cup of coffee in with them, and some were even taking advantage of the time to grab a delayed bite of breakfast.

Noah opened the meeting with an announcement about a new member of staff, joining the department, but there was still too much noise going on for Lauren to hear any more than that. To be truthful, with Holly's situation so much on her mind, she wasn't really paying a great deal of attention to that part of the proceedings.

She knew that their consultant, Ross MacFadden, was going to be away for at least another month, and since Matthew Benedict had moved rather sooner than expected to pastures new they had become quite seriously short-staffed.

Although she had been glad to hear that they were finally going to get the extra member of staff they needed, she really didn't know any more than that. She'd been on her day off when the candidates had been shown around the department and didn't expect to recognise the name of the lucky person if she heard it.

Still, she'd find out all about them as soon as they started work together. She had no doubt that Noah

Kincaid would have insisted on the best man—or woman—for the job. The reputation of St Augustine's attracted applications from the best and there was no way that he would trust his precious little patients with anyone less than the best of the best to fill the number two slot.

Today, as usual, there were several cases presented, starting with the pathologist's report on the massive infection that had struck little Michael's fragile system and drained the life out of him.

Lauren had been devastated that they'd managed to keep him going right up until he was ready to finish intravenous nutrition and begin taking normal feeds into his stomach, only for him to develop necrotising enterocolitis.

It was a recognised risk at that stage of the treatment of a very premature baby's fight for survival and they'd been watching out for it. Even so, the onset of the problem had been so swift and so severe that the whole of his intestines had been involved almost before he'd spiked a temperature. When shock had set in, poor little Michael had been too fragile to survive.

As they moved on, the group was as ready as ever to brainstorm about any patients who were giving cause for concern or who just weren't responding as well as expected. Strictly speaking, that didn't apply to little Holly, who seemed to be holding her own at present.

It was the chaos surrounding the circumstances of the child's birth that was her most pressing problem at the moment, and the results of the expected discussion about her unique situation had obviously been worrying Sunila.

Lauren shook her head and glanced towards the end

of the ward and the clear-sided humidicrib, sharing her young colleague's concern for the tiny child who had stolen their hearts in spite of all her problems. She was such a little fighter.

'No decision, yet, Sunila. At the meeting Noah warned that it could take months or even years to sort the court case out.' She smiled grimly when she remembered the pithy expression the cardiac surgeon had used when he'd spoken about the cold-blooded wrangling going on around their little patient.

'But the parents can't just abandon her here, like returning faulty goods to a shop,' Sunila exclaimed in outrage. 'Who's going to look after her? *Somebody* must be responsible. They haven't even visited her. Not once.'

'With all her problems, she'll probably be spending an unfair amount of time with us anyway,' Lauren pointed out gently, silently sharing Sunila's anger but diverting her thoughts to the series of operations that their little patient had to look forward to. It wasn't going to be easy to correct the serious birth defects that threatened her fragile hold on life. And as for the ones that weren't correctable…

'But if none of her parents want her where will she go between operations?' Sunila demanded. 'This is the first time I've come across anything like this, and I don't know what the law is.'

'I don't know whether there *is* a particular law to cover this sort of situation yet, not with surrogacy still being such a grey area,' Lauren said with a grimace. 'But at least we know that if neither set of parents is willing to accept her at the moment there are some wonderful foster-parents who will love her to pieces in the meantime.'

Lauren knew from experience that Social Services often had to liaise closely with the hospital to find families who could cope with the sort of problems sometimes thrown at them.

'And if they didn't love her you would,' Sunila pointed out with a chuckle. 'I think every child in the department knows as soon as they arrive here that they've got a champion in you. You really ought to have a brood of them yourself.'

Lauren smiled and shook her head, murmuring a noncommittal reply before she turned to walk away. She knew she must have said something comprehensible because Sunila laughed, but she couldn't have said what.

All she could hear as she walked briskly towards the other side of her domain was the empty echo inside her head as she tried to force herself not to remember.

It didn't work.

All she could feel as she looked down at Holly, lying quietly in her humidicrib, was the aching emptiness in her heart where once there had been an ocean of love waiting to pour out on her own children. Maybe not a brood of them, exactly, but at least one or two...

She dragged in a shaky breath and glanced around quickly to see if anyone had noticed her distraction. This side of the department held their youngest patients and, with the hospital's policy of welcoming parental involvement in the nursing of their children, there were always several extra bodies scattered around the room.

Luckily, everyone was busy so no one had noticed

the way she'd been clutching the edge of Holly's crib until her knuckles gleamed whitely through the skin.

'No time for regrets,' she murmured under her breath as she deliberately loosened her grip, repeating the words that had kept her going when life hadn't seemed worth living.

She straightened her shoulders and plunged her fists into the pockets of her white coat as she raised her chin a combative extra quarter of an inch, almost as though daring the world to take another swing at it.

She might not have a husband and children of her own, but at least she had a profession she loved and her colleagues and patients at St Augustine's could benefit from her need to nurture.

The sound of the telephone intruded on her thoughts and she glanced up in time to see Sunila, beckoning her over.

'I thought you'd want to know,' she muttered as soon as Lauren was in range. 'That was Sister Denton from the other side, letting me know that we've got less than a minute before they arrive.'

'Who's arriving? From where?' Lauren felt the frown pleating her forehead. 'Is there another patient coming in? I haven't heard anything about—'

'No!' Sunila interrupted hastily. 'It's Noah. They've been over in the other side of the department and he's bringing the new man to introduce him.'

Lauren ignored Sunila's unusual informality of calling the paediatric surgeon by his first name. Noah Kincaid was the last man to stand on ceremony and it was more important that she found out what was going on.

'What new man?' she demanded, then remembered

Noah's announcement at the meeting. 'Do you mean the new resident? Is he starting today?'

Before Sunila had a chance to reply Lauren heard the familiar sound of the ward doors opening.

'Ah, there she is,' said Noah, smiling at Lauren as he led the way into the room. 'Let me introduce you to one of the most dedicated members of our team— the strictly un-hallucinogenic LSD, Lauren Scott-Dakers.'

Lauren smiled in return, knowing he'd only used her full name to tease her. Her initials were usually a source of amusement and most people joined in the joke, but as her gaze travelled over Noah's shoulder to the man following him she felt her expression freeze.

'You weren't here the day we interviewed him so I thought I'd introduce the two of you myself,' Noah continued, apparently oblivious to her reaction. 'Lauren, this is Jack Madison, my new second-in-charge.'

To Lauren it felt as if the bottom had just dropped out of her stomach, and while her heart thudded loudly in her ears her brain refused to come up with a single syllable beyond a whispered '*Jack*...?'

His eyes were the same mixture of blue and grey as ever, but where they had once made her think of glints of sunlight on deep water now they seemed as hard and cold as tempered steel.

'Lauren and I have met before,' he said quietly, almost dismissively.

If Lauren hadn't been watching she would never have seen that his surprise at seeing her had been as great as her own. As it was, she knew that the blaze of shock and anger in his eyes certainly didn't match the lack of expression in his voice.

As quickly as it had appeared, the emotions were gone, hidden behind a careful screen of dark eyelashes and steely control. But Lauren knew what she'd seen and was left feeling as shaken as if she'd only narrowly avoided being struck by lightning.

What on earth was going on? What was the matter with the man? They'd hardly parted amicably—he hadn't even bothered to say goodbye to her before he'd walked out on her—but surely that meant that *she* had more right to feel aggrieved than he did.

'You didn't say that you knew anyone in the department when you came for interview,' Noah said, clearly surprised. 'I thought you were a newcomer to the area.'

'I am,' Jack confirmed, looking away from Lauren as he answered.

It felt almost as if she were escaping from the jaws of a vice when he released her from his gaze.

She let out a shaky breath, suddenly aware that she must have been holding it ever since she'd realised who her new colleague was going to be.

'We did part of our training at the same hospital,' he was continuing calmly, every vestige of emotion apparently banished, as if he were commenting on nothing more important than the weather.

A sudden surge of anger tore through Lauren, and she barely managed to prevent herself from confronting him. How *dared* he treat her as if she had meant no more to him than a meaningless fling?

At the last second common sense came to her rescue when she realised that *that* was probably the way he remembered her. It had been blindingly obvious from the way he'd treated her at the time that those precious days when she'd known she was falling in love with him hadn't meant the same to him. It couldn't have or he'd never have left her the way he had—

The sound of Noah's pager broke into her thoughts, and when he broke off his conversation with Jack to hurry to the phone it left the two of them standing together.

For several seconds the silence stretched between them in a chasm as unbridgeable as the Grand Canyon as she tried to think of something to say.

'What made you apply—?'

'I didn't realise it was you—'

They both began speaking at once and each broke off to gesture for the other to continue.

The sight of his lean hand just inches away from her bare forearm tightened a hidden knot inside her, as did the memory of the way they'd often managed to speak at the same time. She'd once happily thought that it had been evidence that the two of them had been so in tune with each other that they'd belonged together...

'I was only going to say that I didn't realise it was *you* I was going to be working with,' he continued when she made no attempt to accept his offer to go first.

'Noah *must* have told you about the rest of the team when you were here for your interview,' she exclaimed in surprise. 'How could you *not* have known?'

'How was I supposed to know that Dr Scott-Dakers was once called Lauren Hamilton?' he pointed out with maddening logic. 'The last I heard you'd thrown in the towel at the hospital and gone back to live with Mummy and Daddy.'

The scorn in his voice brought a flare of heat to her cheeks but there was just enough truth in his words to prevent her denying them—at least here in the ward where any number of people could overhear what they were saying.

A quick glance over her shoulder told her that she was wise to be wary. Sunila was hovering near the desk, her dark eyes travelling avidly between the two of them.

Lauren stifled a groan.

She didn't need three guesses to know what the main topic of conversation was going to be the next time the two of them were alone together. And with Sunila's tenacity, she wouldn't like to guess how much she'd worm out of her, given half a chance.

She shuddered when she thought of the hospital grapevine, spreading the story of her past relationship with Jack Madison. If she were to tell anyone about the shoddy way he'd treated her, she had no doubt that within seconds there would be two opposing camps, arguing about the rights and wrongs of the situation. It wouldn't matter to any of the gossips that the 'facts' always grew with the telling and became twisted out of all recognition in the process.

Anyway, no matter what the rights and wrongs of the case, if they were going to be able to work together she was going to have to force her bitterness back into the dark corner it inhabited in her mind. If she didn't it would probably grow teeth and devour her from the inside—

'Is your husband a doctor?' Jack asked, the harsh tone in his voice dragging her attention back to his stony expression with a jolt.

A swift image flashed across her mind of Adrian's

face—not the devil-may-care charmer who had spent so much of his childhood teasing her and pulling her hair as he'd dared her to keep up with his mischief. The picture that haunted her was that of the pale, thin imitation he had gradually become after their marriage.

A pang of guilt mixed with her regrets as she shook her head.

'No,' she said quietly with a reminiscent smile. 'Adrian never did understand what I liked about the profession right from the first time I took care of him when he broke his arm, falling out of our tree.'

The mental image of her childhood friend's mortification when the sight of his own broken limb had made him sick to his stomach had been a bone of contention between them ever since. He'd never been able to accept the fact that a mere *girl* had been able to take charge of the situation while he'd been close to fainting.

'Ah.' The single sound was full of a wealth of meaning and hardly needed the chill in Jack's wintry eyes to underline it. 'He was the scion of one of the local landed gentry, no doubt.'

'Next-door neighbour,' she elaborated briefly, angry that she sounded defensive when there was no need. 'We grew up together.'

Silence fell between them again and Lauren suddenly realised that this time Jack was going to leave it up to her to break it.

'Jack, we need to talk…' she began, calculating the possibility of grabbing some time to speak to him and wondering where they could find the privacy, but she never got the chance to continue.

'Jack, they need us down in Casualty,' Noah announced as he strode towards them. 'A minibus full of children has just arrived and they're all being sick at once.'

'Do you need me too?' Lauren offered, sparing a lightning glance around the ward. She hadn't had time since the meeting to speak with the parents, hovering over their babies, but if there was an emergency...

'I'll call you if we do,' Noah confirmed. 'If you could finish doing the round up here and see what you can get Sister to organise in the way of beds, just in case we need them...'

His last words reached her over his shoulder as he began to stride towards the door.

Jack paused a second longer, the dark arches of his eyebrows drawn into a frown. For a moment she thought he was going to say something—perhaps suggest a time and a place for their long-overdue discussion—but at the last moment he shook his head and turned to follow Noah out of the room.

Lauren found herself breathing a sigh of relief as the doors swished closed behind him, her last view of him through the inset safety glass windows only serving to remind her how tall he was and how broad his shoulders were.

As if she'd ever forgotten!

Jack had been the first and only man she'd ever loved, the man who'd taken her heart and ground it into the dust... She suddenly realised where her thoughts were taking her and snorted quietly in disgust at herself.

Such melodramatic thoughts weren't like her. She was far more likely to be honest with herself and admit that she'd been utterly captivated by his lean, intense masculinity the very first time she'd seen him.

It had been her own fault that she'd been so naïve as to think he'd fallen in love with her too.

She schooled herself to make an orderly round of her charges, taking time to reassure the worried parents that all was going as well as could be expected. At least that was true today, with no unexpected crises threatening to bring desperation to their hearts while each waited to find out if their precious child would survive.

The trouble was that it wasn't enough just to keep her hands busy. There was one complete section of her brain that was functioning on automatic as it scrolled through an emotional recall of the past.

She fought the wry twist to her mouth when she remembered the breathless anticipation she'd felt when she'd heard Jack tap on her door the first time he'd arrived to take her out for a drink.

He'd actually invited her for a meal and then discovered that he couldn't afford it. She'd been tempted to offer him the money, afraid that he would take back the invitation, but one look at the proud jut of his chin had told her it would have been a mistake.

'How about a glass of lemonade and two straws?' she suggested, grinning nervously up at him and hiding her crossed fingers in the depths of her pocket.

'Done!' He chuckled aloud, his eyes glinting down at her and making her feel warm all over. 'An understanding woman. I knew there was a good reason why I was going to love you.'

She knew he was only joking but the precious words wrapped around her heart and she hugged them fiercely to herself during all the long hours they had to spend apart.

He was two years ahead of her and the pace of their

work frequently kept them apart, especially when he was doing nights and she was stuck on days.

She was thrilled that he seemed as eager as she was to spend every free moment together, the warmth of his welcome as he wrapped her in his arms like a balm for the loneliness she felt when there wasn't time to meet.

When he suggested that the only way for their relationship to work was for the two of them to move in together she threw all her scruples to the wind and asked him to help her pack.

Lauren remembered the mixture of laughter and excitement which had infused her as they'd emptied her belongings into an assortment of suitcases and carrier bags. The excitement had run molten along her veins but it had gained a touch of apprehension when she'd let herself think about the fact that she'd just tacitly agreed to them spending the night together for the first time.

Her cheeks burned when she remembered how gentle and considerate he'd been with her, guessing from her nervousness that this was all new territory for her. Her heart started to thump heavily when the memories took a leap forward to the following days and weeks when he'd taught her that gentle seduction wasn't the only face that love-making could wear...

'Lauren...? Hey, Lauren, are you all right?'

Sunila's worried voice finally penetrated her absorption and she whirled guiltily to face her.

'I'm fine, Sunila. Just thinking...'

She had to let the sentence die away uncompleted. There was no way she could tell anyone about her X-rated memories—especially now that the person who'd starred in those memories would be working here.

'Is there a problem with one of the children?' the younger woman queried, her fine, dark brows pinching together in concern.

'Not at the moment,' Lauren reassured her.

'Then you must have been thinking about our new colleague,' she guessed with a sly grin.

'New...?' For a moment Lauren was at a loss. Her mind hadn't been concentrating on the fact that Jack was a new member of staff, just the fact that she'd never expected to see him again, let alone here.

'Oh, *please*!' Sunila exclaimed. 'You can't tell me that you stood talking to him for all that time and didn't notice that he's the best-looking man to come in here in ages. What's the matter with you? Where are all your feminine urges when an eligible man appears? Are your hormones in hibernation?'

'I hadn't really thought about him as being eligible,' Lauren said honestly, an unexpected hollow feeling opening up inside her when she thought about the years that separated Jack and herself. Had he continued to play the field, breaking hearts wherever he went, or had he finally found the special woman he'd been looking for and settled down? A sharp stab of pain lanced her when she realised that he could even have several children by now...

'I'm sorry, Lauren,' Sunila said hurriedly when she realised that her friend wasn't joining in her teasing. 'I forgot for a moment that you're not in the same situation as I am—still looking for the right man. I mean,' she interrupted herself, 'you're not in the market for that first big relationship...'

'Sunila, if I were you I'd stop before I swallowed

both feet,' Lauren teased, drawn out of her unexpectedly painful imaginings by her friend's embarrassed
attempts to save the situation she'd created. 'It's a
very simple story. I was married and my husband died
so now I'm a widow, and I'm not really interested in
looking to replace him.'

'But—'

'That's not to say…' she continued, knowing what
Sunila was going to say—she'd said it often enough
since the two of them had become friends. 'That's not
to say that I can't appreciate a good-looking man,
without wanting him for myself.'

'He *is* good-looking, isn't he?' Sunila grinned. 'All
lean and muscled and moody-looking, and then he
smiles and his eyes twinkle and it's like…like a flash
of sunshine. He's certainly going to brighten the place
up a bit.'

The telephone rang while Lauren was still trying to
control the sudden surge of possessive jealousy which
had shot through her at the thought that Sunila had
been looking appreciatively at Jack—especially the
fact that she'd been the recipient of one of his smiles.

'It's *him,*' Sunila said with a cheeky grin, holding
the receiver out towards her. 'He wants to speak to
you.'

'Hello?' Lauren cursed the breathy sound of her
voice and forced herself to concentrate, not on his
well-remembered voice but on the message he was
giving her.

'Lauren, we've got eight of them here who've all
been accidentally inhaling carbon monoxide from a
faulty exhaust,' he said swiftly, obviously completely
unaffected by the fact that they were working together
again for the first time in nearly five years. 'They're

not too bad, but they all need admitting for a while for observation. What can you do?'

'Annie Denton, the sister on the ward, has commandeered the day room as an interim measure to keep them separate from the rest of the ward. There isn't room for an influx that size over there anyway, and we didn't know at the time whether they'd got something contagious,' she replied equally calmly, detailing the preparations being made over on the other side of the department where the older children were cared for.

Simple pride made her determined that he would never know that he still had the power to make her pulse race with just the slightly husky sound of his voice.

'How many of them will be all right just to curl up in a chair—or will all eight of them need a bed?' she continued. 'We've got two beds empty, possibly three, so any more than that...' She let the sentence trail away, knowing he would understand.

'They're all on oxygen and a couple of them are still being sick so we'll need to cater for that, but otherwise they'll be all right just to curl up in the room together,' he confirmed.

'How long before they're on their way up?' she asked, needing to know how much longer she'd have to make certain that everything was ready.

'About fifteen minutes, I reckon, by the time we get all the paperwork sorted out. Their teacher is going frantic about notifying the parents what's going on.'

Lauren told Sunila what was happening to put her in the picture. She groaned.

'It'll be bad enough to have eight of the little darlings, all feeling rotten in the same small room, but if you get two parents turning up for each of them it's going to be chaos,' she predicted darkly. 'You wait and see.'

'It's a good job Sunila isn't here or she'd be saying "I told you so" by now,' Lauren groaned to the young staff nurse, Julie Thomas, several hours later when the first of the children were escorted out of the ward by their parents. 'It's not as if I hadn't seen it happen before, but never quite on this scale.'

'I must admit this is the first time it's ever been this bad,' Anne Denton admitted quietly as she joined the two of them. Even *her* usually immaculate dark blue uniform was looking a little rumpled. 'We occasionally get the odd hysterical outbreak from a parent who can't cope with the traumas her child is going through, but that lot...' She shook her head as though lost for words for a moment.

Lauren pinched the bridge of her nose between her finger and thumb, hoping that the hovering headache would decide to go away now that the day room's occupants were starting to leave.

'I know we didn't really have any options, but in hindsight I think it was a mistake to put all of them in together like that,' Anne added. 'When that stupid mother suddenly started shrieking and wailing that her daughter could have died she set the whole lot of them off. I've never heard such a noise.'

'I just wanted to smack her,' Julie Thomas admitted with a giggle. 'That's what I used to do to my little brothers when they started that sort of attention-seeking nonsense. It soon brought them back to their senses.'

'Unfortunately, we aren't allowed to use such measures,' Anne said, determinedly trying to keep her 'sister's face' straight. 'Much as we'd like to sometimes,' she added wickedly.

'Well,' Lauren exclaimed, squaring her shoulders with a tired sigh, 'that sort of morning is almost bad enough to make me wonder why I became a doctor, except it's a bit too late to change my mind now. I'm too old for a paper round, too young for a pension and too tired for an affair with a rich man.'

'Well, that pretty well covers all the options,' Anne said with a gurgle of laughter, her eyes drifting beyond Lauren's shoulder to focus on the person who had just entered the ward behind her. 'On second thoughts,' she muttered in a cheeky, low-voiced aside to her superior, 'how wealthy do you think Dr Madison is? His looks are certainly good enough to make me forget about the money and concentrate on the affair!'

Her heart full of dread, Lauren whirled to find that, without her hearing him come in the room, Jack had come to a halt just a couple of paces behind her. When she remembered what she'd joked about she could have groaned aloud. Surely he hadn't been here long enough to hear what they'd been talking about.

It only took one glance at his stony face to tell her that he'd heard every word and had clearly put his own interpretation on them.

He and Noah had been in and out of the ward all morning and Lauren had begun to wonder if fate was playing a particularly malicious trick on her. It seemed as if, within minutes of meeting each other for the first time in nearly five years, she and Jack were fated to be thrown together at every opportunity.

As if it weren't bad enough that her eyes seemed to stray towards him at every opportunity, given the cramped situation in the little day room, they'd ended up rubbing more than elbows as they'd bent over their charges to monitor their progress.

As far as she was concerned, the most worrying part about it was the ever-increasing awareness that flooded through her whenever they touched.

It had been like this when they'd first met, but with the heartbreak of his desertion she'd thought it would have died.

No such luck.

It seemed that all he had to do was glance in her direction and every nerve started to hum, and when he brushed against her, no matter how innocently…

She could feel the heat rising in her cheeks as she turned to face him, and had to stifle her impatience with herself when his expression proved that he was no more affected than if she were just one of his patients.

In fact, he'd probably be looking a great deal happier if she *were* one of the children.

As it was, she'd come to realise during the course of the day that it was only she who was still affected by those long-ago emotions. *He* certainly wasn't having any problem with them.

She'd only been having a joke at her own expense when she'd joked about being too tired to have an affair with a rich man, but from the expression on his face he thought even less of her for even contemplating the idea.

CHAPTER TWO

LAUREN noticed that at some stage during the morning Jack had swapped the jacket of his smart charcoal-coloured suit for a white coat.

She had to smile when she saw that already the pockets were bulging with the usual paraphernalia of stethoscope, formulary, pens and notepads sporting drug-company logos. She carried a similar assortment herself.

For a moment the sight of him, all lean and fit and virile, was so achingly familiar that it seemed as if time had stood still and nothing had changed...but it had.

Lauren forced herself to meet his eyes and, mindful of their audience, found a polite smile.

'How's it going? Are you settling in all right?' she asked, silently congratulating herself that, in spite of the unavoidable tension inside her, her voice sounded perfectly normal.

The laser-like intensity of Jack's gaze and an infinitesimal twitch of his eyebrow told her that he wasn't so easily fooled.

'I'm just wondering whether it's always as chaotic as this or if this morning's effort was specially laid on so that I had to dive straight in at the deep end?' he demanded, throwing a grin towards Julie so that she knew he was joking.

'Oh, it was specially arranged,' Lauren declared

with an answering chuckle, appreciating his attempt at humour. 'We had to see what you were made of.'

'I hope you'll let me know if I pass the test, then,' he said dryly.

'Oh, you've passed with flying colours already,' Julie declared. 'When that youngster stood toe-to-toe with you, arguing about the necessity for coming to the hospital in the first place, and then threw up all over the sleeve of your jacket, we knew you were going to fit in when you reached out to grab a bowl and comforted her without a word of complaint.'

'I was grateful that it was only the jacket that caught it,' Jack said ruefully. 'At least I could replace it with this.' He flicked the lapel of his white coat with one lean finger. 'If it had been the shirt and trousers as well, it could have ended up being a bit more embarrassing because I haven't finished unpacking yet. I might have ended up walking around the hospital in my pyjamas.'

You never used to wear pyjamas...never used to wear anything at all, Lauren thought, unable to prevent her eyes flicking over his lean length as the words flashed into her head.

Heat surged up her throat when she suddenly realised that he was watching her, and she forced herself to look away quickly, trying to find something that needed her attention without making it obvious.

'Are you moving into hospital accommodation?' Julie asked, the gleam of interest unmistakable.

Lauren felt the sharp twist of unwanted jealousy when she watched her younger colleague glow under Jack's attention, but she could hardly blame her. In spite of the painful history between Jack and herself, she still wasn't immune to the pull of his masculinity.

Part of her wanted to move away so she wasn't forced to listen to the getting-to-know-you conversation between the pretty staff nurse and the new doctor in the department. It was the other, more dominant part of her, which desperately wanted to know more about him, that held her within earshot.

'No. We've managed to find something temporary to rent within easy distance of the hospital while we take our time, looking for something to buy for the long term,' he explained.

'We?' Julie questioned, and Lauren could have hugged her. The thought that he was about to talk about his wife and family was like a rusty dagger to her heart, but for some crazy reason she needed to know.

There was a pause and Lauren suddenly knew that he was going to find some way of avoiding an answer—the way he had always avoided talking about personal details when *she'd* first tried to get to know him.

As the silence stretched out for several more seconds she couldn't stop herself from glancing towards him, wanting to see the expression on his face.

She wished she hadn't when she saw that, far from concentrating on his conversation with Julie, he was actually looking at *her*, his eyes utterly devoid of warmth.

'My family,' he said cryptically when the silence had gone on so long that Julie was beginning to look as if she wished she'd never asked.

It was almost comical to see how quickly all the eagerness left Julie's eyes when she realised that, far from being an available bachelor, he was actually a family man.

Lauren seemed to be the only one who wanted more detail. Who had he married? Was it Carolyn? She'd certainly thought she was a far better match for him than two-years-junior and green-as-grass Lauren, and had done everything she could to persuade him of the fact. Did his bare words 'my family' include children as well as a wife or were there just the two of them?

She had no right to know the answers to those questions and there was no way she was going to find out, without asking him herself. Even then she didn't think he'd tell her, not if the closed expression on his face was anything to go by.

The clock on the wall above the desk caught her eye and she realised with a sudden lift of her heart that she was now free to go home.

'Well, if you'll excuse me, I've come to the end of my shift and I've got two hungry mouths, waiting for me to come home and feed them,' she announced brightly. 'See you tomorrow.'

She went to turn away, carefully avoiding meeting Jack's eyes, but his hand shot out and came to rest on her sleeve just above her wrist. She froze, suddenly aware that although they'd been working closely together all morning this was the first time he'd deliberately touched her.

The fabric of her white coat was thick and still stiff with starch but she could feel the weight and warmth of his hand clearly as it rested there.

As if he'd realised that he'd been touching her too long, he whisked his hand away and shoved it deep in his trouser pocket, his bunched knuckles showing clearly through the fine dark fabric.

'I need to have a word with you, Lauren. Just a few

questions. Have you got time before you rush home?'
he said quietly.

His tone was perfectly polite but once again Lauren
was aware that other emotions were seething in the
depths of his eyes.

She bought a little time by glancing at her watch
but it wasn't really necessary. They both knew they
were going to have to talk at some stage, and the
sooner the better if they were going to be able to work
together without this tension between them.

The only thing holding her back was her fear that
whatever Jack said would rip open the wounds that
had never properly healed.

A little voice deep inside her pointed out that their
conversation might just provide the means of allowing
the wounds to heal once and for all, and she gave in.

'We could go and get a cup of coffee or something,
if you like,' she offered, all too aware that Julie was
still nearby.

'My first chance to sample hospital cuisine,' he said
with a wry twist of his mouth, and gestured for her
to lead the way.

They walked in an edgy silence to the bank of lifts
and when the one travelling their way arrived it was
almost full. For half a second Lauren contemplated
waiting for the next one but a guiding hand at her
waist ushered her forward and he stepped in beside
her.

'There's room for everyone if we all breathe in,'
called someone at the back as the doors swished
closed, and several others chuckled.

Lauren was so aware of how close Jack was that
she wondered if she'd ever be able to breathe normally again. At one side she was right beside a wheel-

chair and the doors were behind her so she couldn't inch any further either way to give herself some breathing room.

The lift lurched into action and Jack quickly slung one long arm across her back and grasped her shoulder firmly to stop her from landing in the wheelchair.

She glanced up at him and realised that his innate chivalry had made him angle his body to act as a buffer between her and the rest of the lift's occupants.

Their eyes met and held, his gleaming more grey than blue under the artificial light. She tried to read the host of expressions flickering there as he searched her own in return, but they were too complex for simple analysis. It was almost as if the two of them were isolated from the rest of the lift's occupants by some sort of glass screen, part of their surroundings but separated from them.

Whatever the truth of the situation, she still felt as if he enveloped her, his lean body almost surrounding her as he stood as a bulwark between her and the rest of the world. From shoulder to thigh she was plastered against his body and on every inch of her skin there were nerve endings, tingling with awareness. Even her pulse and breathing were affected and her eyes started to close as the familiar mixture of soap and male musk filled her head with erotic memories.

'Our stop,' he murmured, his voice suddenly jerking her out of the semi-trance that had begun to overtake her.

The doors slid open and she stumbled as she pivoted swiftly to step away from him, almost desperate to put a few inches between them.

With lightning reflexes he caught her by the elbow

and saved her from the embarrassment of measuring her length in the corridor.

'Where's the fire?' he murmured as they set off side by side along the corridor, his long stride easily keeping pace with her hurried one.

Flustered by her clumsiness, Lauren reached for the first thing she could think of to say.

'I don't want to be too late back,' she said, glancing at her watch as if every second was precious in an attempt to hide the heat in her cheeks.

'Ah, yes. The hungry mouths, waiting to be fed,' he said as they joined the queue, his tone noticeably cooler. 'Just one child so far?'

For a split second the thought of having a child, waiting at home for her, was such a painfully sweet one that she couldn't think what he was talking about and her confusion must have shown.

'You said there were two people waiting for you,' he explained patiently. 'I presumed you meant your husband and child.'

His assumption that, much as she'd always longed for a family of her own, she could so quickly and easily have gone on with her life after the way he'd treated her—after the way *life* had treated her—was like a blow.

Pain and regret flooded through her, taking her breath away, but there was no way she was going to let him know how much he could still affect her.

'No husband, no child,' she said quietly, as she placed a small packet of biscuits on her tray beside the cup of tea, doubting that she'd be able to swallow any of it past the boulder-sized lump in her throat. 'Just two very demanding, very spoiled cats.'

She carefully chose a table as far away from any

other members of staff as possible because she had absolutely no wish for their private business to become fodder for the hospital grapevine.

There was a strange feeling to the silence between them as Jack followed her, and she couldn't help watching him from under her lashes as he unloaded from his tray the meal he'd chosen and settled into his seat opposite her. He picked up his cutlery but then made no attempt at starting to eat.

'What happened to the husband, then?' he demanded suddenly, his dark brows swooping into a fierce frown as he leant towards her.

'Husband?' she parroted, disconcerted by the wave of anger he emanated.

'Mr LSD,' he said mockingly. 'You remember? The double-barrelled man you ran off home to marry? Didn't he turn out to be rich enough either? Did you run away from him too?'

Lauren was stunned by the series of assumptions and accusations Jack had managed to fire at her in the space of a couple of sentences, but it was her deep-seated feeling of guilt that made her address the most important one.

'He died,' she said baldly, her brain too scrambled to come up with any other way of telling him, in spite of her years of practice at imparting unpalatable truths.

'Oh, God, I'm sorry,' he murmured, his genuine compassion obviously overruling any other considerations. 'When? How?'

'A year after we were married,' she admitted through a throat thick with anger—anger directed mainly at herself. 'They tried to spare his parents' feelings by calling it an accidental death... What's the phrase? ''Death by misadventure''? But we all knew it was bound to happen one day.'

'What did he do? Race fast cars? Climb mountains?' Jack prompted.

'All that and more, and all to excess, but it was the drugs that finally did it,' she said hollowly. She couldn't ever escape the weight of guilt that it had been her fault that Adrian had needed the spurious emotional prop of illegal chemicals, flirting on the edge of destruction until one day he went too far.

'Drugs?' There was disbelief in his voice and he'd barely managed to keep the volume down. 'What sort of drugs?'

'Expensive ones... Initially, what they call designer drugs, but they weren't enough and he quickly progressed to cocaine and heroin—at least, that's what they found in him when he died.'

'Did you try to get help for him or did he manage to hide what he was doing until it was too late?'

'He hid it at first but...I've always felt that he *wanted* to be found out. At any rate, he didn't want help—unless it was help, finding the next supply— and I was the last person he'd accept help from. Not that his parents will ever believe that, nor mine. They both blame me.'

'What do you mean? How could *you* be to blame?'

'You'd have to know them to understand their particular brand of logic.' She gave a bitter laugh that came out more like a sob. 'As far as they're concerned, if I'd been a proper wife to Adrian and stayed at home, I'd have been a steadying influence and he'd never have gone off the rails in the first place. And, anyway, if I *had* to be selfish and be a doctor, I should have been able to cure him.'

'Catch 22,' he murmured. 'Damned if you do and damned if you don't.'

'Exactly.' Lauren drew in a deep breath and let it out slowly while she drew her control firmly around herself again. Somehow his quick understanding and compassion had taken the edge off her overwhelming guilt. 'Anyway, that's old history now. It all took place before I came to work at St Augustine's, and, as far as I know, only Noah has heard the whole grisly story.'

Her attempt at light-heartedness was almost drowned out by the insistent bleep of a pager. They both looked down to check but it was Jack's that was flashing.

Lauren felt guilty about the burst of relief she felt that they would have no more time to talk. Bringing up the subject of Adrian's death always left her feeling raw, and at that moment all she wanted to do was scuttle off home and lock the rest of the world out.

'I should have eaten when I had the chance,' Jack grumbled as he pushed his congealing meal away and got to his feet. For a moment he paused beside her and she froze, her locker keys clutched tightly in her hand. 'We still need to finish clearing the air,' he said finally, obviously torn between what he wanted to do and where he needed to go. 'Look, I'll have to catch up with you later…perhaps tomorrow?'

'I'll be in just before eight,' she confirmed, and could have kicked herself when she saw him nod before he leant across and grabbed the unopened packet of biscuits off the table in front of her, flashed her an unrepentant grin and strode away.

'What did I have to go and tell him that for?' she grumbled, as she replaced his virtually untouched meal on his tray, adding her cup of cold tea to his cold cup of coffee before she stood up. 'Knowing him, he'll be there, waiting for me to set foot through the door to continue the discussion.'

She thought about her certainty of how Jack would behave on the way back to her flat. Granted, it had been years since she'd last seen him, but she doubted that he'd lost any of the 'take-charge' potential which had characterised him when they'd known each other before.

If he wanted to finish the discussion with her and she said she'd be arriving just before eight, he'd be ready and waiting to speak to her at just before eight.

'If I hadn't told him what time, I could have sneaked a cup of coffee to bolster my spirits,' she was muttering as she let herself into her little ground floor flat.

At the sound of the safety chain, sliding into position, she was greeted by a grumbling chorus of muted yowls and purrs as two rather disreputable-looking cats hurried towards her on silent paws.

'Hello, you two,' she said as she slid her jacket off and slung it over the back of the nearest chair, before scooping them up, one on each arm. 'Did you really miss me or was it only my tin-opening expertise?'

She carried them through to the compact kitchen, relishing the deep, vibrating purrs emanating from the pair of them as she cradled them and ruffled their fur.

As ever, the problems of the day seemed to recede just a little bit and she determined not to think about the hospital and anything connected with it—including Jack—for the rest of the evening.

'Tomorrow morning will be quite soon enough for that,' she said aloud over the sound of renewed complaints as she forked unidentifiable fishy-smelling glop into two bowls and put them in opposite corners of the kitchen floor.

The routine was comforting and it wasn't the first time that she was grateful for the brainwave that had sent her to the nearest animal shelter to adopt an animal.

'Why I ever abandoned my original intention of getting a sweet, innocent, little kitten and came home with you two, I'll never know,' she complained as she stood guard between them.

Desperate Dan and Jack the Ripper were a battle-scarred pair of reprobates who'd been destined for lethal injections the next day when she'd seen them.

Bedraggled and miserable, there had been something in the expression in their eyes that had called out to her. Perhaps it had been the uncanny echo of the same lost and hopeless feeling she'd sometimes seen in her own eyes or perhaps it had been the thought that in just a few hours they would be dead.

Whatever it was, she'd ended up taking the two of them home that same day and had discovered that, although they lived together quite amicably the rest of the time, mealtimes could degenerate into a fight to the death if she wasn't there to act as referee.

It had been sheer whimsy which had led her to give them their less than complimentary names, and it certainly wasn't very helpful when she was trying to shut another Jack out of her thoughts.

'So much for not thinking about him,' Lauren groaned, her temper beginning to fray as she parked her little compact car in the staff car park and tried to get out, without releasing her seat belt.

She didn't usually drive the short distance to the hospital but this morning there'd been no time for the soothing habit of a brisk early morning walk.

To her disgust, after a largely sleepless night she'd finally succumbed to exhaustion around dawn and had slept through her alarm. If the cats hadn't obeyed their internal clocks and come looking for breakfast, she'd probably still be asleep now...

'And I bet he's checking his watch every thirty seconds,' she muttered as she hurried up the stairs, bypassing the queue for the lifts.

She'd learned in the first couple of days of knowing him that one thing Jack was scrupulous about was punctuality. If he said he would be somewhere at a certain time, you could set your clock by him. Unfortunately, it also meant that he didn't have much patience with people who didn't keep the same rules.

A punctual person herself, it hadn't caused Lauren any problems when she'd started going out with him, but she'd seen him blister strips off tardier junior colleagues. She wasn't relishing the thought of being in the firing line even though it would be perfectly justified.

She pushed her way through the ward doors, her mouth already open to begin apologising as soon as she saw him, but there was no sign of his lean, commanding figure anywhere on the ward.

'Hey, Lauren, you're late this morning. That must be the first time since you came here,' noted Sunila as she glanced up from changing Holly's minute disposable nappy.

'Don't remind me,' Lauren groaned as she joined her beside the humidicrib, her eyes looking automatically for any tell-tale signs that Holly needed any extra help. 'Has Dr Madison been looking for me?'

'Don't know. Haven't seen him since I came on duty,' she said with a shrug. 'As far as I know, there's nothing major going on down in Accident and Emergency—at least, nothing paediatric. Have you tried the other side?'

'Not yet. I'll try there next. In the meantime, any problems you want me to look at while I'm here?' She'd pulled on a disposable glove and couldn't resist reaching in a gentle finger to stroke the dark, silky strands that had started to cover the little head.

'Dr Kincaid was up here during the night to have a look at Holly, but apart from that…'

'Holly?' Lauren froze, her anxious gaze sharpening as she examined the little baby. 'What's the matter with her?'

'He's not quite certain, but her monitors keep tripping.'

'Did he say what the most likely cause was? Did he put anything on her chart? What's he decided to do about it?' Lauren knew she shouldn't have favourites but there was just something so special about this little scrap of humanity…

'At the moment we're just keeping an extra-close eye on her, but if it *is* her heart that's causing the problem he said he might have to do the operation much sooner than he wanted.'

'But she's still so small!!' Lauren exclaimed, before she realised she was saying the words aloud, her fears for the child every bit as keen as if Holly had been her own.

'How risky is it?' Sunila asked, the question suddenly reminding Lauren that *she* was the doctor.

'At her age and weight, pretty bad, even with a first-rate surgeon like Noah doing the operation,' she admitted honestly. 'Ideally, she needs enough time to put on a bit of size and strength, especially as premature as she is. But if she's starting to have problems…'

'She could be getting weaker rather than stronger if we wait,' Sunila finished for her.

A high-pitched electronic bleep suddenly shrilled over the various background chirps and peeps of the state-of-the-art monitoring equipment, and both of them glanced automatically towards Holly.

This time it was one of the other babies, and they watched as the nurse specialling him reached in and flicked the bottom of his foot sharply with her finger.

She paused a moment, watching her charge closely, before she reached up to reset the alarm.

'He stopped breathing again,' she reported matter-of-factly as she recorded the incident on a chart. 'Sometimes he goes for hours now, without it happening. I think he's finally getting the hang of this breathing lark.'

Lauren found a smile as her pulse settled back to normal.

'Well, if that's the excitement over for the moment I'll see if I can track Dr Madison down. I'll be back to do a round as soon as we've finished the meeting.'

'That should give us time to get the next set of samples off to the lab and get ourselves organised,' Sunila said. 'In the meantime, if we need you I can always bleep you on your pager.'

'Anytime,' Lauren agreed with a smile.

The smile had slipped a little by the time she reached the other side of the department, and a squadron of butterflies was practising manoeuvres in her empty stomach when she thought about the meeting ahead of her.

Not only was she over an hour later than she'd said, but she was also dreading the topics Jack was going to raise.

It wasn't that she had anything to feel guilty about—not as far as Jack was concerned, anyway. It was the emotional pain she was worried about when she finally heard him tell her in words of one syllable why he'd left her the way he had.

'Is Dr Madison here?' she enquired of the second-year nurse, hurrying towards her with a covered bed-pan in her hands.

'Which one is he?' she asked, her expression slightly frazzled. 'I'm sorry if I sound stupid but I only started on this ward this morning and I haven't put all the names to the faces.'

'He's tall—about six feet—with short dark hair and—'

'I don't believe it!' the young woman interrupted with an incredulous laugh. 'You're not going to tell me that he's a genuine tall, dark, handsome doctor, are you? I thought they only existed in fiction.'

Lauren chuckled. 'Now I know that you've only just started on this ward. You obviously haven't met Dr Madison or his blond counterpart, Dr Kincaid, or you wouldn't be scoffing at the idea of good-looking doctors. We seem to have cornered the market in them.'

'Why, thank you, Lauren, on behalf of both of us. Who said that eavesdroppers never hear any good of themselves?' said a laughter-filled voice, and she whirled to find Noah and Jack standing behind her.

Noah was obviously enjoying her pink-cheeked embarrassment as she introduced him to her young companion, but Jack's reaction was more difficult to decipher.

He was perfectly polite to Amy Protheroe and probably sent her off with her heart fluttering madly when he threw her one of his potent smiles. In between the banter, though, Lauren kept finding his eyes on her, their expression as guarded as she'd ever seen them.

The dark shadows which had appeared under his eyes since she'd seen him yesterday made her wonder exactly how much sleep he'd had in the last twenty-four hours, but, knowing that he was married, that was a topic she wouldn't touch with a barge pole.

'I'm sorry I was late this morning,' she volunteered hastily, deciding to take the bull by the horns rather than wait for Jack to rebuke her for poor time-keeping.

Noah had arranged to spend some time with the two of them in the neonatal intensive care unit against the time he would be needed to leave them in charge while he flew off to the next conference.

They were following in Noah's wake on their way to the unit, and it was no accident that Lauren had chosen this moment to speak. It would take them less than two minutes to arrive at their destination, and with Noah within earshot Jack was unlikely to have the time or the inclination to make much of it.

'I was just going to say the same thing,' he said wryly. 'I only got here about twenty minutes ago myself and I was worried I'd left you hanging around. You've got better things to do than that.'

The fact that Mr Punctuality had been late was surprise enough, but the thought that he'd been worrying about letting her down was even more of a shock.

This was the man who'd spent more than half of their recent time together glaring at her as if he'd have liked nothing better than if she'd disappeared off the face of the earth, and the rest doing little more than tolerating her. Now he was apparently being as considerate as if she were a valued colleague. What was going on?

'When Noah's finished talking us through the unit and bringing me up to speed on the methods he likes to use here I'll be ready for a very large coffee,' Jack continued, as they shouldered their way through the doors. 'I've been up since four this morning and didn't have time for any breakfast. Would you like to join me?'

The tired smile he offered her was completely different to the grin he'd bestowed on Amy, but Lauren suddenly realised which expression was worth receiving.

The grin Amy had been delighted to receive had been little more than an expected social nicety, whereas this time he'd actually allowed her to catch a glimpse of the real man she'd once known.

'I slept through the alarm this morning so I'm running on empty too,' she admitted candidly. 'If you make that a large mug of tea and a bacon sandwich or two, you're on!'

The next hour was almost as intensive as the worst nightmare exam, with Noah throwing information and questions at the two of them with the speed of a machine-gun.

Halfway through Lauren realised that she and Jack had slipped into a once-familiar pattern, each of them sparking off the other's unusually keen intelligence as they alternately absorbed facts and ideas and expounded on them.

'I'm so glad my instincts were right,' Noah exclaimed with some satisfaction when he drew the session to a close. 'I wanted to make certain that I was going to be leaving the unit in good hands when I have to be away, and I had the feeling that the two of you would work perfectly together.'

To Lauren's eye his expression was positively smug, and she would hate to be the one to tell him that his 'dream team' still had a few problems to sort out between them before their collaboration could be considered anywhere near perfect.

'Well, I'll leave you to your quest for the perfect breakfast,' Noah announced, with a quick glance at his watch. 'I promised my wife I'd be home inside the next ten minutes to take her out on a special shopping spree.'

He paused a moment and Lauren was intrigued by the hint of colour that stained the cheeks of their usually very self-contained boss.

'Special occasion?' she prompted, little guessing how his answer would resurrect the unhappiest time of her life.

'Actually, yes,' Noah admitted, obviously bursting to tell someone the secret he was bottling up inside. 'We're going out to choose furniture for the nursery. Helen had a routine scan yesterday and, quite by accident, we found out that we're expecting a daughter.'

CHAPTER THREE

'I PRESUME Noah meant that, quite by accident, they found out the sex of the baby rather than accidentally finding out about her existence,' Jack murmured as they hurried towards the beckoning smell of food. 'You'd think that a man in his speciality would know about such things.'

Lauren was immeasurably grateful that he was there to drag her out of the dark hole into which she'd been about to disappear. It was ironic, really, that the man who had been largely responsible for her misery should now be the means of temporarily lightening the burden, even though his own expression was more frown than smile.

'I presume it's their first,' he continued a few minutes later as he began to attack a large plate of 'cholesterol special' cooked breakfast with gusto.

'Yes and no,' Lauren mumbled around her first bite of a perfect bacon sandwich. 'His wife already had a little son, Nash…gorgeous little chap…' Her voice trailed off for a moment when she remembered the day Nash had visited his father in the department, his dark eyes huge when he'd seen the unit where he'd had his own operations.

Lauren remembered the trusting way he'd allowed her to lift him up so that he could see the tiny babies through the glass, without going into the unit, and remembered the wonderful, sturdy, healthy feel of his little body in her arms.

'He must be nearly old enough to go to school now,' she continued hurriedly, snatching another bite while she tamped down the dreadful feeling of emptiness and loss which could so easily overtake her if she let it. 'He's one of Noah's former patients... needed a couple of rounds of major heart surgery...transposition of arteries, like Holly up on the unit.'

Lauren finally ran out of things to say and subsided into silence, suddenly realising that the conversation had died because Jack hadn't contributed for several minutes.

'Jack?' she prompted when he continued to concentrate on his meal, apparently intent on finishing the whole thing without stopping to breathe. 'Is something the matter?'

'Nothing new,' he said ambiguously, his voice curt as he finally looked up at her.

Lauren had just picked her cup up but when she saw the cold accusation in his eyes she almost lost her hold on it.

'Jack? There *is* something wrong, isn't there?' It took both her hands to steady the cup as she placed it carefully on the table. 'What is it?'

'It never ceases to amaze me,' he began musingly, for all the world as though he were starting an esoteric philosophical discussion. 'You see it so often, don't you? The people who spend all their time talking lovingly about other people's children and taking care of other people's children, but when it comes to the nitty-gritty of taking care of their own...

'I'm just glad for the sake of the human race that there are a few like Noah who actually live up to their ideals and are willing to accept other people's children as well as their own. As for the mothers who don't want their own children…'

By the time his diatribe ran out Lauren was shaking all over.

She had no idea what had set him off. She'd never seen him like this before and really hadn't a clue what he was talking about. She certainly had no idea why he was glaring at her as if whatever had upset him was all somehow her fault.

Unless…

Unless he'd somehow found out what had happened to her five years ago. Had he found out what she'd been forced to do when he'd abandoned her like that? Did he think she should have tried harder to contact him? Did he blame her that she hadn't let him know about…?

Something in her rapidly shifting expressions must have registered with him.

Was it the desolation and fear bound up in past events or the emptiness that had surrounded her ever since she'd realised that she would never be able to fulfil her dreams?

Whatever it was, he must have realised that his vehemence was inappropriate because his expression changed suddenly and he leaned his elbows on the edge of the table and cradled his face in both hands with a groan.

All at once, Lauren remembered him saying that he'd been up since the early hours of the morning.

'Bad night?' she queried quietly, only too willing to forgive his testiness. She wasn't feeling much better herself after a night without much sleep.

'Danny was ill in the night…well, the early hours,

really,' he muttered, and abruptly had to stifle an enormous yawn.

'Danny?' she echoed faintly, wondering if that was his wife's nickname and dreading finding out.

'Yes, Danny,' he repeated with a renewed edge to his voice as the upper half of his face emerged from behind his hands to reveal those forged-steel eyes. 'My son.'

As Lauren stared at him she wouldn't have been surprised to find that her heart had stopped beating or her lungs had stopped needing to draw in air.

His son! Jack had a son!

Suddenly she was hit broadside by a wave of emotions. There was overwhelming anger that, after the way he'd failed her, he'd so easily been able to go on with his life—to marry and have a child—but the strongest emotion was a desperate jealousy that his child hadn't also been hers...*theirs*.

It took several slow calming breaths before she could speak.

'What's wrong with him?' Pride alone kept her voice under control, her tone no different than if she were holding the same conversation with any of her colleagues.

'I'm not sure, other than the fact that he's been sick several times,' he mumbled, as he propped his chin in his hands, his head apparently too heavy to stay up on its own. 'His temperature isn't even raised. All he can tell me is that his tummy hurts and he doesn't feel well. He only had his first day at pre-school yesterday.'

The voice emerging from behind his curled fingers was full of the same frustration she'd heard many times from other parents, only in his case the fact that he was a doctor meant that there was extra pressure.

'He probably can't tell you any more than that,' she pointed out logically. 'It could even be something as simple as being over-tired or getting over-excited by all the changes in his life. How old is he?'

There was a strange silence before he straightened to face her directly, his expression suddenly strangely wary.

'Danny's four,' he said, as if she should somehow have known, his voice as sharp as the assessing look in his eyes as he stared at her for several very long seconds.

She had begun to feel very uncomfortable under his scrutiny by the time he broke the silence.

'You don't really care, do you?' he murmured in apparent amazement, his words making no sense at all to Lauren. 'How can you do that—just put things out of your mind and go on with your life as though none of it ever happened? You just seem to sail easily through life, making certain that nothing ever touches you very deeply.'

Before she could protest he'd straightened to his feet with a speed that shot his chair noisily backwards, drawing several pairs of eyes in their direction.

'I'll see you around,' he said dismissively, and strode away as if he couldn't bear to be in her company a moment longer.

It was her turn to bury her face in her hands as she tried unsuccessfully to sort through all the thoughts whirling in her head.

What on earth had got into the man?

One moment they were discussing his son and she was suggesting possible reasons for the child's illness and the next he was implying that she was hard and unfeeling and didn't really care about her patients.

Ha! That showed how well he knew her, she thought sadly. There had been many times since she'd started her training as an idealistic eighteen-year-old that she'd lain sleepless in bed, worrying about one of her little charges, and many tears she'd shed when, despite their best efforts, they'd lost one.

And all because she'd never been able to find that essential distance between the part of herself that was the doctor and the part that was a woman.

She'd never met Jack's son, Danny, so she couldn't relate to him as an individual. Nevertheless, she cared deeply that a little child was sick and hurting and didn't know why.

If Jack couldn't remember that much about her then he had no right to cast aspersions.

She was still seething when she went back up to the ward, and it took some heavy-duty concentration while she explained procedures to the parents of their latest admission before she put the unhappy scene behind her.

Young William was his parents' pride and joy, and it was obvious that his 'little problem' was the cause of considerable anguish to them.

From what Lauren could gather, the child's father had met his mother in America in the course of their high-profile jobs. Both of them sounded as if they tended to set themselves impossible goals and then drove themselves into the ground, trying to achieve them.

'I just don't understand why this has happened to us,' William's mother complained in her rather nasal American accent. 'As soon as I realised I was pregnant I paid for the very best pre-natal care. Our little Willie shouldn't have had *any* imperfections.'

'Especially not in that…department,' blustered his father, his face flaming with a mixture of embarrassment and indignation. 'There's been nothing like… that…happen on either side of the family before. We checked very thoroughly.'

Of course, Lauren was sympathetic towards their worry and confusion—any operation on a child, even a relatively minor one, was so traumatic to a parent— but the first time she heard the nickname the poor child had been saddled with she was hard-pressed to keep a straight face. The American diminutive was nothing short of disastrous, especially in view of his problem.

'Well, you can never tell when something like this is going to happen,' she soothed. 'If you were to think about the thousands of stages and millions of cell divisions involved in the development of a baby from a single cell to birth, it's amazing that *any* of them arrive without anomalies.'

'I suppose,' the mother agreed grudgingly. 'And I suppose we should be grateful that at least it's something hidden. If it had been something wrong with his face…a harelip…' She shuddered as though unable to contemplate anything worse.

Lauren couldn't help her eyes straying towards the wall that separated the little interview room from the ward. Out there any number of parents would be delighted if their seriously ill child had something as minor as William's problem instead.

'That's all very well for you to say,' the husband butted in, 'but when he eventually goes to prep school the other boys will give him hell if his…thing…isn't the same as theirs.'

'The surgeon is very good at his job,' Lauren pointed out. 'William had the preliminary operation to correct the severe downward curvature when he was one, and it was completely successful. Now it's time to complete the repair of the abnormality in the urethra by—'

'Don't!' begged William's mother with a little shriek as she put her hands over her ears. 'Don't tell me any more. I can't bear to think about it.'

'All *I* want to know is whether it's going to look normal when it's finished,' her husband muttered, as if he, too, was having difficulty with the conversation.

'How many different versions of normal are there?' Lauren challenged, staring him straight in the eye. 'I've seen a lot of them since I started my training at eighteen and I've never seen two of them exactly alike.'

'You know what I mean,' he blustered. 'Little boys get more chance to…to compare than girls. Will it look like mine?'

Several wicked quips about the fact that Lauren hadn't had the privilege of seeing his and therefore she wasn't qualified to comment on the relative dimensions between a four-year-old and an adult male leapt to her tongue but she managed to resist them all.

'One of the reasons for doing the surgery when they're young is so that they can develop as normally as possible, both physically and emotionally,' she replied seriously. 'That means that he'll soon be able to learn to pass urine, standing up, like you, and as he grows his development should be similar to yours.'

'And will it…er…perform normally when he gets older, too?' he muttered, this time unable to meet her eyes at all.

'As far as I know, it will have all the usual functions—including reacting to a pretty girl,' she added euphemistically, knowing that was what he was really asking.

By the time Lauren ushered the two of them back to the ward to rejoin their totally unconcerned son in front of the television, all she could think about was finding a large mug of coffee.

'Phew! That was hard work. I'm in desperate need of caffeine, Annie, preferably intravenously,' she announced, as she pushed the ward sister's door closed behind her. 'Is there any water in the kettle?'

She turned to find Anne Denton on the phone, one hand raised in a holding gesture.

'Just a minute, Mrs Madison. One of the other doctors has just come in. If you wait a minute I'll ask her,' she said, and covered the mouthpiece.

Lauren stood stock still at the sound of the name, the rest of the words washing straight over her at the realisation that Jack's wife was on the other end of that phone line.

'Lauren, do you know where Dr Madison is? I've tried paging him but he hasn't got back to me yet. Apparently his son hasn't been very well and Mrs Madison is sounding a bit frantic.'

'He said Danny was ill during the night,' Lauren confirmed. 'I take it this means he's worse?'

'He's in pain and being very sick—can't even keep water down. She's worried he's going to become dehydrated and they haven't had time to register with a

GP yet so she doesn't know who else to turn to. Poor little chap, I can hear him crying in the background.'

'If you've tried to page Jack...' Lauren paused while she weighed up the possibilities. 'I'll try to find him, but in the meantime I think it would be best if Mrs Madison brings him straight in. If he's just got a serious stomach upset and he's bordering on dehydration we can do something about it, but if it *is* something more serious he'll be in the right place for that, too.'

'Right.' Annie gave her a thumb's-up sign and turned back to the phone. 'Mrs Madison? Have you got a car there?' she began, as Lauren hurried out of the office and started towards the other end of the department in search of Jack.

She finally ran him to ground as he bent nearly double over a new addition to the premature baby unit while he tried to insert a needle into a vein no thicker than a piece of cotton.

'Come on, now, sweetheart, help me out here,' he crooned half under his breath, as he tried to perform the manoeuvre with the minimum of contact with the child's tissue-fine skin to lessen the risk of damage.

His hands looked huge against the child who looked less than twelve inches long, her little limbs no thicker than his fingers and her skin almost transparent.

'Got it first time,' he announced in a voice full of satisfaction, and straightened to strip off his mask with one hand while the other remained to assist in stabilising the line while it was taped into position.

'Who's the newcomer?' Lauren asked, knowing there hadn't been any problem deliveries in progress last time she'd heard.

'One of twins,' Jack said briefly. 'Mother didn't realise she was in labour until it was too late to halt it—thought it was last night's curry, apparently.'

'And the other one?' Lauren glanced around but couldn't see another newly occupied humidicrib.

'Couldn't get him started,' he said gruffly. 'And this one's going to be touch and go before we know if she'll make it.'

Lauren felt the familiar bands tighten around her heart when she heard about a child dying at birth. It was such a cruel thing to carry a child for so many weeks, only to lose it as soon as it emerged into the world.

'Lauren?'

Jack's voice dragged her out of her painful thoughts and she suddenly remembered why she'd been looking for him.

'Your pager,' she said. 'Annie's been trying to get hold of you and you haven't answered.'

'Dammit! I forgot,' he muttered with a scowl. 'It went off while I was working on the other twin in the delivery room.'

'And you drop-kicked it to the other side of the room?' she suggested, knowing how impatient he could get when interrupted in the middle of something important.

'Something like that,' he admitted wryly. 'Did someone send you out to track me down? Is it urgent?'

The way his eyes kept straying from the tiny figure in the cot to the various displays on the monitors told her how involved he was with his latest little charge.

'I don't know how urgent it is, but I thought it was important. There was a phone call from your wife, saying that Danny's getting worse. She's worried that he might be getting dehydrated so—'

'Oh, God. Danny!' he exclaimed, as he whirled towards the door, obviously fully prepared to drop everything for his son. 'What did she say? Does she want me to come home?'

His eyes were flicking rapidly between the tiny baby, the door and herself, as if he was torn between his love for his son and his duty to his patient.

Instinctively, Lauren reached for his arm to offer him comfort, but the warmth of his skin was almost shocking against her palm and it took a conscious effort to keep it there.

'Jack, she didn't know what to do for the best so I told her to bring him here as soon as she could.'

'She's on her way in? Bringing Danny?'

Lauren nodded and under her hand she felt the tension ease out of him.

'Annie took the call so I don't know any details, such as whether she was going to drive,' Lauren began, only to be interrupted when he shook his head.

'She doesn't drive and, anyway, I've got the car here. There wasn't time to walk this morning—'

'In which case, Annie will have told her to get a taxi. There's a company based in the hospital forecourt who are well used to ferrying patients to and fro. They'll probably be here in a matter of minutes so if you want to go down to meet them I can hold the fort up here—'

The words were hardly out of her mouth when there was a disturbance outside the unit that couldn't fail to draw their attention.

'Dad-dy!' wailed a little voice, clearly audible

through the closed door, and Jack strode off urgently across the room.

Lauren followed in his wake, filled with a strangely morbid fascination. Part of her wanted to stay as far away from Jack's perfect little family as possible—it could only hurt to see all the things she had once wanted for herself and to know that she could never have them.

The other part of her couldn't resist taking a quick look at Jack's son—the son *she'd* hoped to give him one day.

The fact that she was about to meet the woman he'd married was just the payment she'd have to make for seeing—

'He's burning up, Lauren,' Jack said, whirling to face her with his son in his arms as she came out of the room to join them. 'Feel him. He's far too hot.'

'How hot?' Lauren retorted automatically, trying to cover up the shock of her first sight of Danny.

He was such a perfect miniature of his father that it had momentarily taken her breath away.

He had the same high cheek-bones and slightly pointed chin, the same broad, intelligent forehead. Even his colouring was right, from the slightly olive tone of his skin and dark close-cropped hair down to the softly curled eyelashes, lying over the upper curve of his flushed cheeks.

'What?' Jack sounded distracted as he curved his powerful body protectively over his vulnerable burden and touched his lips to his son's forehead again.

'Give me a figure, Jack,' Lauren demanded crisply, and was pleased to see that her tone had snapped him out of the beginnings of panic. 'What *is* his temperature?'

'I don't know,' he admitted, and straightened. 'Can you get me a thermometer?'

'Better than that, why don't you carry him through to the little interview room and have a proper look at him?' she suggested.

By the time she joined them in the interview room he had already begun to strip off Danny's pyjamas and Lauren was glad she'd thought to grab a fresh pair for the little lad.

'Here…' She offered him the thermometer, guessing that he would want to take care of his son himself.

He took the child's temperature, and when Lauren saw the expression on his face she knew it was high. Before she could ask exactly how high Jack prepared to check the youngster's blood pressure, but Danny gave a little wail and began to struggle in his father's arms.

'Shh, shh, Danny. It's Daddy here. You're going to be all right. Stay still just another minute, son.'

'Uh-oh,' Lauren muttered, when she caught a glimpse of the sweaty little face, and held a bowl out towards him.

'Well held,' Jack muttered, as Danny retched painfully, his stomach obviously empty.

'He's been doing that ever since you went to work this morning,' said a voice behind them, and Lauren suddenly realised that there was another woman in the room and she hadn't even registered her presence.

'How much has he been bringing up?' Lauren asked, as she turned to face her, and paused in surprise.

The woman in front of her was wringing her hands with worry and, from the size of it, it was obvious that she'd just thrown one of Jack's jackets over her quietly elegant clothes to come out of the house—but who was she?

She couldn't be Jack's wife—she was at least a couple of decades too old. Likewise, there was no way she could be Danny's mother.

'He's been bringing up less and less,' she confirmed, her soft voice clearly concerned. 'He keeps saying it hurts his tummy and makes his throat sore, but he can't even bear to take enough water to rinse his mouth and throat out, without retching again.'

'Has he eaten anything that could have disagreed with him?' Lauren asked, concentrating on trying to work out what was wrong with the little chap rather than working out who this woman was.

'He hasn't had anything that I haven't had with him,' she declared stoutly.

'Not even at school?' Lauren prompted. 'What about his school meal?'

'He doesn't have them yet. He's only going to school part time until September when he'll go full time,' the older woman explained. 'He came home for his dinner at midday yesterday.'

Lauren threw a glance at Jack, expecting him to ask a few questions of his own, but it was almost as if he had abdicated his role of doctor in favour of concentrating on being a parent.

'Has he been passing water normally?' she asked, wondering if the problem might be referred from a urinary infection or even a stone blocking a duct.

'He wasn't complaining of any pain right up until the last couple of hours, but he doesn't seem to have been going so often. Then, he hasn't been drinking anything so there probably isn't as much going through him, is there?'

'Jack? How are his bowel sounds, and have you checked McBurney's point?' she demanded in a sudden flash of intuition.

'McBurney's?' His head came up, his eyebrows drawn into a sharp frown. 'He's only four. Surely he's far too young for appendicitis?'

'Come on, Jack,' she chided. 'Stop thinking like a father and think like a doctor for a minute.'

There were several seconds of surprised silence before he chuckled briefly.

'Point taken,' he conceded with a sigh, and directed his attention to the unhappy child, lying limply on his lap. 'Let's have a look at you, sweetheart. Can I have a feel of your tummy?'

'No, Daddy. Don't. My tummy hurts,' Danny moaned, trying feebly to flap his father's hand away.

A sharp cry a couple of seconds later told them both that Lauren's guess had been right.

'Can you phone to get the theatre organised?' Jack asked, as he straightened carefully out of the chair, his own face several shades lighter as he had to listen to his son, whimpering in his arms. 'I'll take Danny straight through to wait.'

'You'd do better to wait in here until I let you know everything's ready,' she pointed out, and hurried off, without waiting for a reply.

The theatre list for the day had already finished when Lauren arrived with her request for immediate theatre time.

She didn't know why, but some strange intuition was telling her that even though Danny had been sick for less than twenty-four hours his case was far too urgent to wait for the next scheduled list.

Within minutes she had persuaded two of the

nurses to prepare the theatre for Danny's arrival, and while everything was being set up she put a call through to Noah to ask him to perform the surgery.

Her explanation of her strange sense of urgency didn't surprise him at all but presented a problem where he was concerned.

'There's no way I can get there in time—I'm too far away,' she heard Noah say, the reception on his mobile phone crackling in her ear. 'If you're convinced it needs to be done straight away, get on and do it. I've no doubt at all that you'll make a first-class job of it.'

His whole-hearted endorsement was music to Lauren's ears, and by the time Jack carried Danny through to the anaesthetic room, with an IV already in place to counteract dehydration and the bag of fluid draped over his shoulder, she was already gowned and scrubbed.

'I'll only need a couple of minutes to get ready,' he said, when Danny had succumbed to the anaesthetic and Jack had laid him gently on the trolley.

'No, Jack,' Lauren said quietly. 'We're going to start straight away.'

'But I want to—'

'I know you want to help him,' she interrupted swiftly, 'but it's really not a good idea. Besides,' she persisted, when it looked as if he was going to continue the discussion, that strange sense of urgency growing stronger with every passing second, 'I don't think Danny can afford to wait even that long.'

CHAPTER FOUR

FOR a couple of very tense seconds there was absolute silence in the theatre as if everyone was waiting for Jack to explode.

Lauren held his gaze resolutely and willed him to bow to reason. She hardly dared to breathe until she saw the moment when he gave in, his shoulders suddenly slumping in surrender.

'I'll go and wait with my mother,' he said quietly, and stroked his hand one last time over his son's head before he stepped back to allow the trolley to go through to the theatre.

At the last moment he turned back to meet Lauren's gaze, his own eyes filled with a torment that told her he'd gladly suffer any agony if it would save his son.

'Look after him for me,' he whispered, the words so quiet that she almost had to read his lips. She longed to reach out to him to offer him the solace of human contact, but she'd already scrubbed up and she didn't want to have to take the time to do it all over again.

'As if he were my own,' she promised, and meant every word.

She reversed through the doors, her hands held carefully in front of her so that she wouldn't touch anything, and they swished closed after her as she turned to face the operating table.

It was far from the first time she'd operated on a child this young—with her speciality in paediatrics

61

she was called on to deal with any age and size from premature babies almost up into young adulthood.

Somehow this time was different.

In the instant that she'd seen him for the first time, cradled against his father's much larger frame, little Daniel Madison seemed to have taken hold of her heart. For the first time, seeing a little boy lying so helpless on an operating table in front of her and relying on her to make him well had a very special significance, although she'd have been hard-pressed to put the emotion into words.

'All ready at this end,' said John Preece, his lean, wiry frame settled into the anaesthetist's usual place at the head of the table.

Lauren glanced over her mask at the nurse, similarly garbed to herself, and gave her a nod that she was ready to start.

Mindful of the structural problems that could be caused by badly executed incisions, she kept the cut through the skin relatively small then worked her way down through the various layers of muscles, cutting each one separately in the same direction as the muscle fibres grew as she went.

By the time she reached her goal any slight nervous tremor in her hands had disappeared with her fierce concentration, but the sight that met her eyes was worse than she'd imagined.

'Dear God,' she whispered. 'Will I ever get it out in time?'

'What's the matter?' John demanded, his sharp ears picking her words up even over the sounds of the machinery surrounding him. 'What have you found?'

'He's been ill for less than a day and it's just about

to perforate already,' she said in horror. 'I hardly dare touch it in case it goes.'

The thought of the problems little Danny would have if that swollen appendix let its burden of poison loose inside him was enough to give her nightmares.

For just a second she contemplated calling Jack in to help her—he was far more experienced than she was—but then the thought of asking him to take responsibility for operating on his own son brought her to her senses.

'Here we go, then,' she murmured, as she reached in carefully through the incision and gently curved her fingers underneath the badly discoloured organ.

She didn't breathe properly until she had separated it from the large intestine and dropped it into the waiting dish.

After that the rest of the operation was almost an anticlimax, the careful stitches positioned in each separate layer of muscle going in almost automatically as she revelled in the thought that she'd got to it in time.

In no time at all the anaesthetic was being reversed, and by the time Lauren had stripped out of her theatre scrubs Danny had been taken through to Recovery and Jack was waiting by his side.

'How's he doing?' she asked, as she came to a halt just behind Jack.

He was sitting on one of the ubiquitous stacking chairs, hunched over as he held Danny's tiny hand in his much bigger one. The room was so warm that he was just in his shirtsleeves, his cuffs rolled partway up his arms and his tie completely missing.

When he heard her voice behind him he turned just far enough to allow him to look at her over his shoulder, without releasing his contact with his son.

'A couple of minutes ago he opened his eyes and told me he still felt sick but his tummy had stopped hurting,' he murmured with a faint smile, and Lauren noticed that, in spite of his obvious relief, his colour still hadn't returned to normal.

'Jack, are you sure you're all right?' she asked, concern for him pulling at her whether she wanted it to or not. With Danny waking him up in the early hours of the morning, he'd been tired before the day began, but with the stress of an emergency operation on top of everything he looked terrible.

Without thinking about it, she put her hand on his shoulder and gave it a gentle squeeze, wanting to let him know he wasn't alone in his concern for his son.

'I'm fine,' he murmured, reaching up absently with his free hand to lay it over hers. 'And, thanks to your quick thinking, so's Danny. If you hadn't thought about appendicitis…'

'You'd have got there in the end,' Lauren pointed out honestly, glad that she'd been there to help but knowing that he was too good a doctor not to have thought about the possibility as soon as he'd stopped thinking like a father. 'Your next step would probably have been ultrasound to find out what was going on.'

'But by that stage it would have been too late,' he said heavily. 'I could have lost my son.'

'Oh, Jack. Even if the appendix had perforated before we got it out, we could still have put a drain in and given him antibiotic cover. His recovery would have taken longer but—'

'You obviously haven't had a chance to check up on the status of that thing you took out of him,' Jack interrupted with a wry smile.

'Well, no,' Lauren admitted. 'I wanted to come here to find out how he was doing.'

'He's doing a damn sight better than he would have been if you hadn't spotted it. His appendix was gangrenous by the time you got it out.'

Lauren blinked.

'I hadn't realised it was that bad,' she murmured, a wave of horror flooding through her when she realised just how close Danny had come to disaster. It had been much worse than even she had realised.

It wasn't until her hand tightened reflexively on Jack's shoulder that she found she was still touching him and, more than that, found that his hand was still covering hers.

Her eyes were drawn to the sight, his larger, stronger hand almost hiding hers under its lean strength.

She had a sudden mental image of the first time she'd ever seen that hand touching her naked body, his skin almost bronze as he'd cupped pale flesh that had never been exposed to sunlight.

Heat and tension started to coil deep inside and she forced her thoughts back to the present.

The last thing she needed was for Jack to realise how strong her attraction still was towards him. He'd taken advantage of her once, with disastrous results. She would have to be mad to give him a chance to do it again.

'Well, if Danny's on the mend…' she began, trying to slide her hand out from under his without him noticing.

'Lauren.' He tightened his grip so that she couldn't escape, the serious tone in his voice silencing her nervous words. 'I just wanted to say thank you,' he said quietly. 'What you did for Danny...'

'I didn't do anything special,' she denied hurriedly, finally managing to retrieve her hand and tucking it out of reach by folding her arms. 'It was only a simple appendix, and if it hadn't been your son you could have done it with your eyes shut.'

'There was nothing simple about it,' he said, the contradiction all the more forceful for the quiet conviction in his voice. 'You got to it in time and got it out cleanly, and John Preece said the way you closed him up was a work of art.'

She tried to shrug off his gratitude, but couldn't deny the glow his praise had lit inside her. After all the tension between them since they'd met up again it was like balm to her soul.

'With any luck he should heal faster and have fewer problems with adhesions,' she explained simply. 'The last thing an active young man needs is restricted movement for the rest of his life because some surgeon cobbled an operation.'

'How did you guess about the activity?' he asked, with a wry grin.

'I remember the way you always found it hard to sit and do nothing. He's far too much like you not to be the same,' she admitted, glad that he was lightening the mood.

She saw his expression change, his eyes growing intent as he examined her face, and she suddenly realised that her unguarded words might have revealed far more than she'd intended.

'Have...have you told your mother that he's all right?' she stammered, needing to get away from his analytical mind. The last thing she needed was to give him any more food for thought.

'She knows the operation was a success but not much more than that,' Jack confessed, glancing back at Danny's sleeping form. 'I came to find out the details for her.'

'In other words, you waited with her just long enough for Danny to be wheeled out of Theatre before you shamelessly bludgeoned your way through hospital red tape to be here with him,' she interpreted dryly. 'You knew darned well that ordinary parents wouldn't be allowed near a patient until they'd been transferred back to the ward.'

'OK, I took advantage of my position on the staff to find out how it had gone,' he admitted crossly. 'So take me to court. He's my son and I love him.'

The open declaration of his love for his son turned something soft and mushy inside her. It wasn't many men who would stand up and be counted like that. Certainly not her own father...

'Better than that, I'll go and have a word with your mother so you can stay here,' Lauren offered, feeling a hot pressure behind her eyes as the emotional tears, gathering there, threatened to spill over.

She needed to get out quickly before she disgraced herself—needed to put some space between herself and Jack Madison while she got her emotions back under control.

'Mrs Madison?' Lauren said softly, one hand coming out to hover by the elbow of the sleeping woman as she contemplated waking her.

In the few minutes that they'd been in the same room earlier Lauren hadn't had much time to do more than look at the woman who'd brought Jack's child to the hospital. Then she'd had to hurry off to get things ready for Danny's operation and there hadn't been time for any more speculation about her identity.

All she could really remember was a flood of relief when she'd realised that she wasn't going to have to meet Jack's wife under such fraught conditions. *That* pleasure was still to come…

She hadn't even realised that the tall woman was his mother until Jack had conceded that he'd wait with her while Lauren performed the operation.

In fact, because he'd been so reticent about his background when they'd first known each other, she hadn't even realised that Jack's mother was alive until that moment.

Now that she could take her time, looking at her, Lauren could see that the poor woman hadn't slept properly in days. Or perhaps it was just relief that Danny was going to recover that had allowed her to relax into such deep, healing slumber.

In spite of the evidence that she'd dressed in a hurry, it was still obvious that she was a very elegant woman.

Her clothes showed quiet good taste and her hair, the same dark hue as her son's and grandson's, bore a single swathe of white as the only clear evidence of her age. It was swept into a simple style that showed off the same patrician bone structure as Jack's and her slender hands, a smaller, feminine version of his, were clasped loosely at her waist.

The skin around her eyes and mouth had begun to wrinkle, but Lauren could tell that it was evidence of years of smiling rather than any other cause.

'Doctor?' Jack's mother mumbled, her voice rusty

with the remains of sleep as she struggled to sit up. 'I'm so sorry. I didn't mean to fall asleep.'

'Don't worry, Mrs Madison. It's not a problem,' Lauren said soothingly. 'Waiting around can be very tiring, can't it?'

'And boring,' the older woman agreed as she straightened her skirt and smoothed her hands over her hair. 'It's not as if there's anything much to do to keep your mind occupied while you're waiting for news.'

'Jack told you the operation was a success?'

'In the same breath that he told me he was going to sit with Danny until he's moved up to the ward,' she said wryly. 'Oh, don't worry about it. I'm used to him putting Danny first. He just loves that little boy so much…' She shook her head.

'What about Danny's mother?' Lauren asked, forcing herself to voice the question. 'She must be frantic. Have you been able to find a phone let her know what's happening to Danny?'

'Her!' The older woman's face darkened with anger. 'She wouldn't know Danny if she bumped into him in the street. Do you know, she was going to have an abortion? She wanted to kill my grandson!'

'What!' Lauren was horrified. Someone had wanted to get rid of Jack's son? 'But I thought a woman couldn't have an abortion without her husband's agreement.'

'They weren't married,' she said bluntly. 'Jack only found out about the baby by accident and only just in time, by all accounts.'

'No wonder Danny's so precious to him,' Lauren mused aloud, remembering the way cool, calm Jack Madison had flapped like any worried father when his son was ill, completely forgetting all his specialised medical training.

'He *is* going to be all right, isn't he?' Mrs Madison asked, her own affection for the child equally obvious. 'I'd never forgive myself if I'd left it too late to call someone.'

'Appendicitis can flare up very quickly,' Lauren explained, perching herself on the arm of the chair closest to the older woman to show she had plenty of time to spend with her. 'You do get cases that are called "grumbling appendix" which apparently go on for weeks, but usually the whole thing builds up in a matter of days or, as in Danny's case, just hours.'

'Isn't there a danger that things will happen so fast that it bursts before you can get it out?' Mrs Madison asked with a worried frown. 'I can remember a school friend of mine being off school for weeks when she got peritonitis. She nearly died when hers burst and all because the doctor thought she was putting it on to get out of going to school.'

'It can happen,' Lauren admitted honestly, quelling a shudder when she thought about just how close Danny had come to being one of the victims, 'but there are a few things that have changed since you were at school that help to reduce the risks.'

'I should hope so. If technology has progressed far enough to put a man on the moon I would expect something as common as treatment for appendicitis to have improved.'

Lauren chuckled at her dry comment. She genuinely liked this woman, and under other circumstances she would have loved to have had her as a mother-in-law.

Still, that was all water under the bridge.

'Trust me, it has,' Lauren said. 'There are various new ways of making the diagnosis, including ultrasound and—'

'Ultrasound?' she exclaimed in surprise. 'I thought that was used during pregnancy?'

'Oh, we've found lots of uses for it, especially as it saves us from having to take so many X-rays of children. And then there's a whole arsenal of antibiotics we can use to fight infection if the worst does happen and the appendix perforates before we can get it out.'

'There wasn't much more than penicillin back then, as far as I can remember,' Jack's mother reminisced briefly, before bringing herself back to the present situation. 'You're certain that Danny's out of danger now?'

'The operation went well,' Lauren confirmed. 'We were able to take him straight into Theatre and get on with the job—'

'Once you'd thrown Jack out,' his mother interjected with a tired grin. 'He was spitting nails when he came in here about some upstart woman, taking over.'

'That's me,' Lauren agreed with an answering smile, 'but I don't think anyone would have been very happy with a surgeon operating on a member of his own family, except in extreme circumstances.'

'And unless there was someone competent to do it,' added a familiar voice from the doorway.

'Jack!' His mother's eyes lit up as she rose to her feet. 'Is everything all right?'

'Danny's fine,' he said reassuringly as he walked into the room and wrapped his arm around her shoulders in a companionable hug.

Lauren's heart tried to batter its way out of her chest as his smile encompassed her too, and she had to concentrate as he continued speaking to hear his voice over the thunder in her ears.

'I came down to let you know that he's been moved to the ward so if you want to go in for a quick visit—just to reassure yourself.'

'He's awake already?' Mrs Madison exclaimed in surprise. 'I thought he'd still be affected by the anaesthetic.'

'The new anaesthetic cocktails aren't quite the sledgehammers they used to be,' Jack explained. 'He's been awake but he's still very drowsy. He won't really know you're there for several more hours so you can go home to catch up on some sleep.'

'I've already had some sleep, haven't I?' Mrs Madison turned to appeal to Lauren.

'You *were* asleep when I came in,' Lauren agreed, 'but, honestly, Jack's right. There's no real point in staying now. Danny'll need you far more tomorrow when he's crabby and looking for distraction and entertainment. If I were you, I'd go home and recharge my batteries so I'd got the energy to cope with him.'

The older woman was still loath to believe them, and it wasn't until she finally saw how sleepy Danny was for herself that she agreed to let Jack escort her to the taxi rank in the hospital forecourt.

As the taxi drove away Lauren was suddenly aware that the two of them were standing, watching the tail-lights disappearing, almost as if they were a couple.

'It's time I went home too,' she said hurriedly, as Jack turned towards her, aware of a strange aura of emotional danger surrounding them as they stood in the rapidly fading daylight.

With so much unresolved between them, it would definitely be better for her peace of mind if she kept her distance a little bit and stuck to work-based meetings and conversations.

After all, unless one of them was going to volunteer to give up their wonderful job at St Augustine's, they were going to have to find a way to work together for the foreseeable future...

'Are you sure you haven't got time for a—?'

'I'm due to assist with tomorrow morning's list,' Lauren interrupted quickly, 'and if I'm not bright-eyed and bushy-tailed...'

There was a telling pause and Lauren found herself holding her breath while she waited to see if Jack would accept her clumsy change of topic.

'Anything interesting on the list?' he asked eventually as he matched her pace on the way back up to the unit to retrieve her bag and car keys.

'Well, I'll be watching the reconstruction of Willie's willy for a start,' she said, seizing on the topic like a lifeline. She was soon chuckling helplessly as she gave him an abridged account of the excruciating talk with young William's parents.

'Poor kid. I don't understand how parents can do that to their children, do you?' Jack demanded in disgusted tones. 'William's a good traditional boy's name and there are several perfectly acceptable diminutives. What on earth possessed them to use a common slang word for the very part of his anatomy that was going to need attention I'll never know.'

'Let's hope they don't have a second son with the same problem and shorten his name to Dick!' Lauren suggested, and found herself waiting for Jack's wicked grin.

'It's a bit like the family I met who gave their child the initials E.T. at the height of the popularity of the film!' he countered, continuing the silly game.

'As long as the child didn't resemble the creature...' Lauren commented, with an attempt at seriousness.

'Well, she wasn't bright green, but the last time I saw her she had her mouth wide open and was screaming at the top of her lungs so the physical resemblance was quite remarkable.'

Lauren finally had to call a halt when she was having to stifle her giggles with a handkerchief, but she was enjoying their nonsense conversation so much that she was almost sorry she'd interrupted his invitation to stay a little longer.

The regret followed her home to her lonely little flat just a couple of streets away from St Augustine's, but common sense told her she was being wise.

They'd always enjoyed the time they'd spent together, and had taken things slowly to build up a friendship before they'd finally succumbed to the physical attraction that had sparked like lightning between them.

At least, she'd thought they'd been friends, she reminded herself as she ruthlessly dispelled the fuzzy air of happiness that had dared to collect around her.

She'd actually believed that she'd found her soul mate—the man who would stand beside her, offering his strength when she needed it—but when he'd disappeared out of her life without a word she'd had to rethink a great many of her assumptions.

Having had a poor night's sleep the previous night, Lauren's head had hardly hit the pillow before she was sound asleep but her slumber was fraught with dreams.

At first the scenes inside her head were happy ones, filled with images of her first meeting with Jack, such as their collision with loaded trays which he'd later claimed to have engineered just so that he would have a chance to introduce himself.

The weeks when she'd hurried back to the flat she'd shared with two other medical students as soon as the day was over so that she could be ready to see him had been unexpectedly sweet.

Her schooling at a rather exclusive girls' boarding school had left her with a great deal of knowledge gained from conversations after lights-out but absolutely no practical experience.

Jack's patience and consideration of her need to take things slowly had been unexpected for such an apparently experienced man so that when he'd finally asked her to move in with him the love that had been growing inside her had overflowed in a wholehearted yes.

Her discovery that in spite of Jack's careful insistence on protection she had still become pregnant had shocked her at first, but by then she'd been so certain of their love for each other that she'd had no doubt that together they'd find a way to make things work.

Nervous that she wouldn't be able to find the right words to tell him everything she was feeling, she committed her thoughts to paper.

On her way out to the medical school she propped the envelope in the middle of the table up against the pot of the little barrel cactus he'd bought her, where he'd be sure to see it. He'd had to go into work earlier than her that day and she was counting on the fact that he would be home first so that he'd have time to read it before she got back.

Her hands were clammy with nervousness as she opened the door, the bag containing his favourite take-away Chinese meal weighing heavily on her arm as she wondered what he would say when he saw her.

What she hadn't expected was to come back to an empty flat, the two rooms littered with the evidence that Jack had been in a tearing hurry when he'd stuffed several handfuls of his belongings into a suit-case and left.

She looked everywhere to see if he'd left her a note and had waited endless days for him to contact her, but there was nothing.

She even knocked on the door of the other flat on their floor and asked the rather stunning model who lived there if she'd taken any incoming messages on the communal phone in the hallway, but there'd been nothing.

Finally, when the morning sickness which plagued her almost from the start caused her to lose more than twice as much weight as she could afford to lose, she gave in and phoned her parents.

It was frightening just how quickly they managed to arrange for her old friend and neighbour, Adrian, to travel up to collect her and bring her home.

In the space of an afternoon he helped her to sort out her belongings from the ones Jack had left behind in his rush to go, stacked them in his car and she was on her way out of London.

One last forlorn look over her shoulder at the place where she'd once been so happy was all she would allow herself before she set her face towards the fu-ture...alone.

*   *   *

Lauren was still sobbing when she woke up in the early hours of the morning, her pillow dampened by the tears she'd shed while her subconscious had re-lived the heartbreak of those days.

Because she'd loved him so deeply she couldn't bear to think that he'd willingly treated her so badly, and for a long time she'd tried to find a logical reason for his desertion.

In the end it had been her parents who had sat her down and forced her to accept the fact that Jack had never loved her and hadn't been about to take re-sponsibility for the child they'd created.

It had broken her heart to admit that they were right. She supposed that it was only human nature to cling to illusions until all hope was gone.

The one thing her parents *hadn't* been able to do had been to persuade her to get rid of the baby.

'Tainted blood,' her father roared. 'No decent man will ever want to marry you with another man's bas-tard clinging to your skirts.'

'What about your career?' her mother asked, trying to achieve the same end by subtler means. 'You'll be ruining your life.'

But Lauren had been adamant in her determination to keep her baby. Jack might not want it but she loved it already and if in the sleepless hours of darkness the suspicion crept into her mind that it was just *because* it was Jack's child that she wanted to keep it, the thought was ruthlessly squashed.

Her greatest ally throughout that painful time was Adrian.

Whenever the pressure from her parents grew too much to bear she fled to her room and phoned him just to hear the sound of a voice from happier times.

As her due date drew near her parents suddenly seemed to become more reconciled to the fact that she intended to keep the baby, even booking her into a private clinic where her child could be born in relative comfort and seclusion.

Lauren protested at the unnecessary expense—there was a perfectly good hospital nearby—but when they insisted that they wanted to do their best for her she saw it as the offer of an olive branch and finally agreed.

Even those elegantly exclusive surroundings weren't able to prevent the nightmare that her labour turned out to be.

At first everything seemed to be progressing perfectly normally, if a trifle slowly, but just when she entered the second stage and was finally looking forward to holding her baby something went wrong.

A catastrophic malpresentation, she was told afterwards. They'd had to move quickly to save her life, the doctor said, his eyes looking over her shoulder as if he couldn't bear to look her in the eye.

All Lauren knew was that when the anaesthetic finally wore off she woke to be told that her precious baby had died only moments after the birth.

CHAPTER FIVE

'How are you feeling this morning, Danny?' Lauren asked, as she perched on the edge of the youngster's bed.

She was due in surgery soon, but had deliberately come in a few minutes early so that she would have time to visit Jack's son.

'I stopped being sick, but my tummy's hurting again,' he croaked, his little cheeks still flushed and his blue-grey eyes feverishly bright as he lay propped into a more or less comfortable position by a disintegrating nest of pillows.

'Did you tell the nurse that your tummy's hurting?' Concerned, she reached out to stroke his forehead to check how warm he was, then lingered to smooth the ruffled, silky spikes of dark hair into some sort of order. He was so much like his father...so much like the mental image she'd had of her own child if she'd lived, but in her case she'd softened the boyish angularity of the features and added longer hair...

'I told her at breakfast time,' Danny whispered, his words finishing on a squeak. 'Ouch!'

Lauren realised that he'd started to fidget uncomfortably and she saw his face screw up when the movement triggered increased pain.

'Did she give you anything?' she asked, concerned that the poor little chap might not be getting sufficient post-operative analgesia.

'She didn't give me any breakfast but she put some

stuff in there with a needle.' He pointed to the administration port in the intravenous line, snaking down towards his hand.

'That's good,' Lauren said, giving him a reassuring smile. 'It was the stuff to take your pain away and it should start working in just a couple of minutes.'

'Are you sure?' he whispered, his face screwing up as he concentrated on trying to move slowly.

'Shall I show you how to make it work quicker?' she whispered back, leaning closer to him to make it seem like a secret.

'Yes, please,' Danny whispered, the expression in his eyes making her think of a small trapped animal.

'First of all, if you're uncomfortable you'll find it won't hurt so much to move if you let me help. Do you want me to sort your pillows out a bit?'

'I slid down in the bed and everything's all ruckled up underneath,' he whispered.

'Let's see if we can unruckle it, then,' she offered, and set about pulling the sheets straight and tight and rearranging his gown around his sturdy little-boy body.

'Is that better?' Lauren prompted, and received a wan smile and a nod. 'Now we're going to take the pain away,' she said, and took his free hand in hers.

'Is there a special place that you like to be—better than anywhere else in all the world?' she asked, and when she saw his little face screw up as he concentrated the tight bands around her battered heart loosened just a little bit.

'Not really,' he admitted softly. 'I haven't been everywhere.'

'What about your new house?' she suggested. 'Is

there a room there that you like the best? A place that feels special or makes you feel happy?'

'I like my new bedroom because it's got all my special things in it,' he started hesitantly, 'and I like it because I got a special seat in the window and I can pull the curtains round and no one knows I'm there.'

'What can you see outside the window when you're all cosy and warm in your hiding place?' Lauren asked, deliberately keeping her voice low and soothing while she worded her questions to make him concentrate on the images inside his head.

'I can see all the grass and trees that go on and on instead of just houses, and...and I got trees in the garden, right outside my bedroom window...only they haven't got any proper leaves on them.'

Lauren wasn't certain what he meant, but all the while he was talking it was taking his mind off his pain and giving the medication time to work.

'What sort of leaves *has* it got, then?' she prompted.

'They're all sort of crumpled up, like green paper hankies,' he said, wrinkling his nose endearingly.

'Ah, I think that's just because they're very new leaves,' she suggested. 'I think that by the time you go back home you'll find that they've opened up a bit more and started to look like real leaves.'

'How long will that be?' he shot back quickly, obviously becoming more alert as the misery of pain receded.

'That depends how fast your tummy mends, but probably just three or four days,' she reassured him.

Lauren caught sight of Annie Denton out of the

corner of her eye and glanced across, to see her point-
ing at the watch pinned to the front of her uniform.

Puzzled, Lauren looked at her own watch and was
amazed to see just how much time had passed while
she'd been talking with Daniel. If she didn't hurry she
was in danger of being late.

'How are you feeling now?' she asked, as she
straightened and released his chubby little hand,
strangely reluctant to leave Danny's side.

He looked so small and somehow defenceless, surrounded by the big mound of pillows, that she wanted
to stay to keep him company.

'The pain's nearly gone out of my tummy!' he exclaimed, his voice still slightly husky but filled with
delight. 'How did you do that?'

'That's the special secret—*I* didn't do it, *you* did,'
she told him, and rose, glad to see that the misery had
disappeared from his little face. 'You were thinking
about your special place, and because you were thinking about something that makes you happy that helped
the pain to go away.'

'*You're* not going away, are you?' he asked in a
small voice, the animation leaching away almost as
suddenly as it had returned.

'I've got to go and look after some other children
for a little while,' she explained simply, wondering
why this child out of all the children she'd dealt with
during her medical career so far should make her feel
as if she were abandoning him.

'Are you going to do a noperation to someone
now?' he asked suddenly, his blue-grey eyes uncan-
nily like his father's in their intelligent alertness.

'That's right but, if you like, I could come and visit
you again later on.'

'And Daddy?'

'Oh, I expect your daddy will be visiting you every chance he gets,' she said with a smile, and couldn't help leaning forward to smooth a hand over his silky hair one last time as she said her goodbyes.

William was the first patient on the list that morning and his plastic surgery went well.

'Hopefully, his parents will be happy with the result,' Lauren commented, as the diminutive figure was wheeled out of Theatre and into the recovery room.

To protect their handiwork in the initial healing stages they'd installed a catheter, but as soon as the reconstruction had settled down that would be removed and he would be able to try out his new plumbing for himself.

'His father will probably get the shock of his life when he gets his first look at the post-operative swelling, but everything usually returns to normal pretty quickly,' John Preece commented on his way out to the anaesthetic room for the next patient.

While Lauren stripped off her disposables and prepared for the next case she and Jack held a low-key conversation about the relative frequency of different operations carried out in the unit over the space of a year.

'Appendicitis is definitely the most commonly performed emergency operation everywhere,' Jack commented as he pulled on a fresh pair of gloves. 'Mind you, in my own defence for not spotting it sooner, it *is* comparatively rare at Danny's age. He probably did well to have your little hands working on him. That incision was a work of art.'

'When I saw how close the appendix was to perforation I was wishing I'd made one big enough to get a whole kidney bowl in, just in case it burst,' Lauren admitted, quietly delighted by his approval. He'd thanked her last night, but she'd put that down to gratitude that his son had survived the emergency. His praise today was a different matter.

As John pronounced the next patient ready Jack was already commenting on the fact that the age factor wasn't the same for the occurrence of inguinal hernias as appendicitis.

The next three patients were clear evidence of that fact. All three were boys, about the same age as Danny, and all had presented with a painful swelling in the groin area.

'I know you've only been qualified a few years longer than I have, but when you've done as many of these as you have do you ever get the feeling that you're on a production line?' Lauren joked, as she made an incision close to the third little boy's groin and prepared to repair the tear in the muscle that had allowed a loop of bowel to protrude.

'If I ever did I'd take it as a sign that it was time to retire,' Jack said in all seriousness. 'I don't think it would ever get that bad in this unit because they seem to get tremendous variety here. But it certainly helps if you remember that each operation is of vital importance to the person under your knife. It might be your third in a row that day, like the one you're doing now, but it's *his* first.'

'And you never know when something out of the ordinary might come along to stop you settling into a rut,' John Preece added from his end of the table. 'I remember a set of twins we had in a couple of years ago.' He shook his head.

'That was really eerie. They both presented with vomiting and localised pain, but one was complaining of pain on the left and the other one on the right. We were pretty certain one of them had appendicitis and we thought the other one was having some sort of telepathic "sympathetic" pain for his twin.

'It wasn't till they each had an ultrasound that we found they *both* had appendicitis but that one of them had all his organs in exactly the opposite position to the other.'

'You mean like a mirror-image?' Lauren questioned as she paused in the closing process, glancing up briefly before she concentrated her gaze again on what she was doing.

'Exactly,' John said. 'It was the most peculiar feeling, seeing everything in the "wrong" place. Quite disconcerting.'

'Also incredibly rare,' Jack added. 'And that's not to mention the mathematical chances that both of them would get appendicitis at the same time.'

Lauren straightened from the table and stretched to ease the tension that had built up in her back during the morning's work.

'Finished,' she announced, as she taped a dressing over the neat row of stitches. She pulled down her mask and turned to smile at John. 'He can go through to Recovery as soon as you're happy with him.'

'A good morning's work,' Jack commented. 'I can see what Noah meant when he said that he was really beginning to enjoy keeping you company in Theatre these days. You're getting so good that it's more like a social visit.'

'I'm just very glad that he's been so conscientious about his role as teacher,' Lauren countered. 'It's all very well to learn about the various operations from books and then observe them, but the real test comes when you're doing one yourself and it's not a text-book case.'

She was well into her stride now, having learned soon after she moved to St Augustine's that this was a place where her opinions would be as valued as any of her colleagues'. Not like some hospitals, where a mere junior wouldn't be expected to have an opinion let alone have the temerity to express it.

'There are too many hospitals where the first time a trainee surgeon sees an operation is at the elbow of a colleague just one year ahead of him,' she continued.

'The second case is the one done under the colleague's supervision and the third one is done completely alone and unaided. What's worse, the patient is completely oblivious to the fact that he's being used as a guinea pig,' she added, only too aware that she was very lucky to have been spared that sort of stress.

'Apart from the high probability that accidents will happen with that system,' John Preece butted in, 'the trouble is that any innovations that an experienced surgeon has developed over years of practice are lost because there's no time to pass them on from one ''generation'' to the next. Each new crop of surgeons have to work them out for themselves.

'I must say, I'm far happier with the system at St Augustine's. There's far less stress our way.'

'Some people might feel it's too much like hand-holding,' Jack suggested, apparently supporting the system he'd trained under at their old hospital.

Lauren found she couldn't agree. 'You hold a child's hand while he learns to walk, don't you, so why not when you're teaching such a complicated skill as surgery?' she countered.

'And with that simple logic, I now declare the war over,' John said with a chuckle as he stepped between them. 'I hope it's safe to come out from behind the barricades.'

'How can there be a war when we're all on the same side?' Jack asked, and gestured for Lauren to precede him to the door.

'The only side I want to be on is the *out*side of a large plate of food,' said John, rubbing one hand over an audibly rumbling stomach. 'I'm just going to have a look at all my little patients and wait to make sure they've all woken up nicely then I'm off.'

Lauren had been all right until John had mentioned food but, although she was suddenly starving, once she'd changed back out of her theatre scrubs something drew her back to the ward to see how Danny was feeling now.

She already had a smile on her face, ready to greet her little patient, as she rounded the end of the cubicle, then realised with a start of surprise that he wasn't alone and came to a halt.

'There she is, Daddy,' Danny exclaimed when he caught sight of her. 'I told you she said she'd be back.'

Lauren couldn't help smiling in return when she saw the way his eyes were sparkling with pleasure at seeing her. He was almost a different child from the bundle of misery she'd seen this morning.

'Hello, Danny. How are you feeling now? You look a lot easier.'

'I thought about our special secret when the pain started coming back and my tummy doesn't hurt nearly so much now,' he announced proudly, one little hand hovering protectively over the site of the operation. 'And I haven't been sick *all* morning. Not once.'

'Well done. I think you're very clever.' Lauren was absurdly proud of the way the little chap was coping with such a momentous event in his young life. She'd seen plenty of adults who hadn't handled it nearly as well.

Unfortunately, concentrating on the son hadn't stopped her awareness of the father, sitting silently at his side, and the time came when she had to acknowledge his presence.

'Jack.' She nodded briefly, silently cursing when she felt the heat of a blush start to crawl its way up her throat.

There was something completely different about seeing him like this, rather than working beside him in Theatre.

It wasn't just the fact that he was sprawled comfortably in the chair beside Danny's bed with a book open in one hand, as though she'd interrupted story time. There was something about him that drew her towards him as strongly as iron filings to a magnet.

Would she ever be able to treat him as just another colleague, without this tingling awareness electrifying every cell in her body? Probably not until her mortal remains had been pushing up daisies for a millennium or two, she thought glumly.

'Ah, did you and your mother manage to catch up on some of your sleep?' Oh, why didn't I just keep my mouth shut? she thought in despair when she heard the inane question. After the intelligent discussion they'd been having up in Theatre he'd begin to wonder if she'd removed her brain at the same time as her disposable gloves.

There was an embarrassingly long pause before he replied, and she had ample time to notice that his eyes were hard and suspicious and his face had lost the teasing expression it had worn when he was talking to his son as she arrived.

'I heard you visited Danny this morning,' Jack said, the words sounding suspiciously like an accusation. 'Any particular reason why you've been coming to see him so often?'

Lauren was taken aback. She would have thought that Jack would have been pleased that she'd been keeping a close eye on his little son. Hospital could be a very big frightening place for such a young child.

'You mean, apart from my concern over a patient I operated on yesterday?' she challenged, determined she wasn't going to let him know how his attitude stung.

'Yes,' he replied baldly. 'Surely there's no need for so many visits unless he's in danger of developing post-operative complications?'

'So far there's been no indication of infection and, apart from a rather uncomfortable episode earlier this morning, his temperature and post-operative pain seem to be well under control,' she said stiffly, for all the world as if she were making a report to an over-bearing headmaster.

'So? Why *are* you here?'

'Had it ever occurred to you that people might like spending time with Danny because he's an interesting person to talk to?' she demanded, under the cover of a smile for the child in question.

She'd suddenly noticed the worried frown pulling

together the little eyebrows, which were an exact rep-
lica of his father's, and the fact that his eyes were
travelling between the two of them, like a spectator
at a tennis match, as he followed their tautly con-
trolled exchange.

Luckily, she doubted that anyone else on the ward
had heard anything of their low-voiced exchange, but
she could see that it was upsetting Danny to be caught
between the two of them.

Before she could think of some way to let Jack
know how bad this could be for his son Danny spoke
up.

'I'm sorry, Daddy,' he whispered in a shaky voice.
'My tummy was hurting and she talked to me. She
told me secrets to make it go away.'

'Secrets?' Jack repeated, throwing a suspicious
glance in Lauren's direction. 'What sort of secrets?'

'We were talking about our favourite places,
weren't we?' he appealed to Lauren. 'And I was telling you about my new bedroom and the seat by the
window and the trees and grass and stuff.'

'And the leaves looking like crumpled-up green
hankies,' Lauren reminded him with a smile when he
came to the end of his hurried list.

'And you told me they'd look like real leaves when
I get home again,' he finished triumphantly. 'Did I
remember everything?'

'Everything,' she agreed with an emphatic nod and
when he beamed at her she couldn't help smiling
back.

'See, Daddy,' Danny said earnestly, turning to his
father. 'She said if I think about things that make me
feel happy then it helps the pain to go away, and it
worked.'

'Perhaps she should tell that to *all* her patients,' Jack said, his eyes once more fixed on her.

'Oh, don't worry, she does,' Lauren said with a smile for Danny, amazed to hear how steady her voice was when Jack's strange attitude towards her had her emotions in turmoil. 'Now, if you don't mind, Danny, my tummy's rumbling so loud the nurses are going to wonder whether there's a thunderstorm coming.'

Danny's happy chuckle at her nonsense made it worth the effort, and with a wave and a casual farewell she left the room.

The main doors at the other end of the department had started to swing closed behind her when they were suddenly flung open again with great force.

'Just a minute,' Jack hissed through lips held so tight that they were nearly bloodless. 'I want a word with you.'

'I beg your pardon!' Lauren whirled to face him in disbelief, her heart pounding with the rush of adrenaline.

Who was this man, chasing after and snarling at her like a rabid animal? There wasn't a sign of the good manners he'd always shown when she'd first known him.

'Oh, stop pretending that butter wouldn't melt in your mouth,' he sneered. 'We both know what's going on here.'

'Well, if you think *you* know, why don't you tell me because I haven't a clue,' she retorted.

Suddenly the tension between them had reached such a pitch that she knew she had to say something.

'Oh, come on—' he began, but the words boiling up inside her couldn't wait.

'About five years ago we met during our training.

I fell in love with you and thought you felt the same way about me so, when you asked me to, I moved in with you.

'Big mistake,' she said derisively, mocking herself. 'The relationship only worked when the going was good, but as soon as something went wrong...' She shook her head. 'You didn't even bother to tell me you weren't going to be around any more. I came back from that lecture and you were gone...without a word!'

The ache inside her as she had to relive that dreadful day was as keen as ever, in spite of the years that had passed, and the only way she could contain it was to wrap her arms around herself and hold on tightly until this dreadful confrontation was over.

'That's one way of twisting the facts,' he began, but she wasn't listening.

'Well,' she continued regardless, determined to finish what she'd started, 'I'm not just some inexperienced little medical student now and I don't know what's got you all bent out of shape, but ever since you arrived here you seem to have taken a delight in being as bad-tempered as possible. So, I'm telling you now, until you can keep a civil tongue in your head I'll thank you to stay away from me.'

With that she turned on her heel and stalked away from him along the corridor, her knees threatening to collapse at every step.

'Blasted man,' she muttered under her breath as the smell of food reached her and she realised that she'd completely lost her appetite. 'It's a pity I don't need to go on a diet because I'd have no trouble dropping a stone or two with him around.'

Lauren closed her eyes when she remembered how

much weight she'd lost the first time round and how it had put her pregnancy in jeopardy until she'd managed to find something her stomach would accept.

She'd always been slender, even as a child, but the years of ballet training her mother had arranged for her after school had given her a strength and stamina way beyond her appearance.

She'd had good reason to thank her mother for it because there was no way she could have even contemplated training as a paediatric surgeon unless she'd had incredible reserves.

As it was, she was aiming for a consultancy and by the time she got there she was going to be one of a very tiny minority of women in a very male-dominated speciality.

If she didn't starve to death in the meantime, she thought as she turned back again and made herself pick up a tray and contemplate the choices on the menu today. She would need her health and strength to follow her career, and no man was going to get in the way of it—not a second time.

The long day was over at last and Lauren had actually managed to stay completely out of Jack's way since their confrontation outside the unit.

The trouble was, although she was ready to go home, she somehow couldn't contemplate the idea of going away, without saying goodnight to Daniel.

'Oh, for heaven's sake,' she mumbled, when she found herself peering cautiously around the curtain to see if Jack was with his son. 'It's becoming some sort of second-rate French farce, with everyone skulking around trying not to bump into each other.'

Daniel was alone, his head turned towards the mur-

mur of the television set, but Lauren couldn't tell whether he was interested in the programme or was just using it as moving wallpaper. Perhaps he'd already gone to sleep?

'Have you got time for a visitor?' she said quietly as she stepped round the curtain.

There was a slight frown on his face as he turned towards her, but as soon as he saw who his visitor was he beamed.

'You came!' he exclaimed, carefully shifting himself against his nest of pillows so that there would be room for her to perch beside him. 'Daddy said you wouldn't have time to visit me much now that my operation is over.'

'Well, you're getting better so quickly that you don't need me to be your doctor any more, but if you don't mind having an extra friend...'

'You can be my best friend in the hospital,' he announced, as he settled himself again then lifted the soft toy cradled in the crook of his arm to show him off. 'And this is my other best friend. Granny brought him in for me so I wouldn't be lonely when I didn't have any visitors.'

'And who's this?' Lauren asked, flicking one very threadbare ear.

'He's Tog-the-dog and Granny gave him to me when I came out of the hospital when I was very tiny.'

'Does he go everywhere with you?' she asked, seeing how battered it was. She imagined him as a toddler, dragging a toy nearly half his size as he staggered along.

'Everywhere 'cept in the garden,' he said seriously. 'I got him all muddy one day and put him in the bath, then he was all wet so I couldn't take him to bed.

Now he sits on my bed and waits for me until I come in again.'

'Very sensible,' she said with a nod, thoroughly enjoying the conversation.

'If I had a *real* dog he could come outside to play with me, but we can't have one because— Hey!' he exclaimed, interrupting himself. 'Daddy said that we couldn't have a dog because we didn't have a garden, but he said when we had a garden we could start looking so's we can find the right one...and we *got* a garden now!'

Lauren couldn't help chuckling at his glee, and wondered how Jack was going to take Danny's announcement that it was time they started the great dog hunt. She could almost feel sorry for the man because she didn't doubt that Danny would be relentless until he got just what he wanted.

A little corner of her heart wished that *she* was going to be going with them while they tried to decide what sort of dog was the right one, but after today she knew there was no chance that Jack would invite her to accompany his little family.

CHAPTER SIX

'SAMMY TOLLIVER'S coming in today,' Anne reminded Lauren as she checked the list of admissions, a steaming mug of coffee in her free hand. She switched her attention to the silent man hunched over in the other comfortable chair. 'Have you had a chance to look at his file, Jack?'

Jack glanced up briefly from his preoccupation with the folder he'd spread open across his lap, his own mug propped precariously on the wooden arm of the chair.

'Got it here,' he said, his tone preoccupied. 'Makes grisly reading, doesn't it, poor little chap? How many operations will this make?' He flicked his thumb down the edge of the thick bundle of pages before he slapped the folder closed again.

'I'm sure he'll tell you when he gets here,' Lauren said with a grin. She'd met Sammy before and knew what a character he was in spite of the brittle bone disease that had blighted his young life.

Her mood today was infinitely lighter than it had been yesterday. She'd been dreading seeing Jack this morning in case the tension spiralling between them spoiled the good working atmosphere in the department.

His initial general greeting to the small group, gathered for an early morning get-together while they went over the highlights of the day ahead, had been a good indicator of his mood. It seemed almost as if he'd decided to call a truce.

Now all she had to do was wait and see whether the truce would only hold when she and Jack were in the company of others.

What would happen the first time he saw her by herself—or, worse still, with his son?

'He'll also probably tell you that the last time he was here he actually had to stay in for a couple of extra weeks because he had another fracture while he was in the hospital,' Lauren continued hurriedly. Her thoughts had wandered so far off the track that she'd completely forgotten the topic of conversation under discussion for several long minutes.

'How on earth did that happen?' Jack looked up from the file, his expression shocked. Brittle bone sufferers were particularly vulnerable but that was why everyone would have been taking extra precautions when dealing with him. Anyway, you didn't often hear of patients suffering extra injuries while they were actually in hospital.

'He was being his usual cheeky self and aimed a mock punch at one of the orderlies,' Annie explained with a grimace. 'Unfortunately, he got a bit excited, forgot to pull his punch and broke his ulna—again. I think it was the twenty-seventh time.'

'Ouch! That's not what he's come in for this time, though, is it?' Jack asked, turning to the most recent set of paperwork.

'No. He's having the tibia and fibula in both his lower legs pinned to prevent any more fractures, otherwise he's going to be permanently confined to a wheelchair. His body is under-sized but even so it's grown big enough and heavy enough that just the weight of it on his legs is enough to cause fractures.'

'His thighbones were done last time, I see,' Jack commented, without looking up from the notes.

'Yes, and when the pins were put in his legs were straightened out a bit.' Lauren chuckled. 'He was delighted to find he'd gained an extra couple of inches in the process.'

'So he's hoping for great things this time, too,' Annie added. 'I don't know if it's really sunk in with him that he's never going to grow any taller.'

'He's hoping that as soon as he's recovered from this lot we'll do his arms,' Lauren said. 'He knows they'll have to be done one at a time so he can still use the other arm, and he knows how much each operation is going to hurt, but he's got his master plan with each stage linked up.'

'He certainly doesn't lack courage,' Jack said quietly, echoing Lauren's own feelings about the youngster.

Sammy was the first patient with brittle bones that she'd had the chance to get to know over a period of time, and it had made quite a difference to her understanding of the effect of the disease on the sufferer.

When he'd accidentally broken his arm last time just when he'd thought he was going to be able to go home she'd seen it at first hand.

She'd been the one who'd had to sit down beside Sammy's bed and tell him he couldn't leave. She'd heard him voice through his sobs his frustration that his bones were so soft that he hardly dared to move in case they broke.

At least each operation was helping to minimise the number of injuries he could suffer to his major bones.

With the metal rod inserted into the centre of the bone, it would also stop the gradual erosion of height which each fracture had been causing.

It wasn't for nothing that children with this disease had been nicknamed 'humpty dumpty' children.

'Who's scheduled to do it?' Jack asked. 'Noah?'

'I think you'll find it's Alex Marshall,' Lauren volunteered. 'He's top orthopaedics man at St Augustine's since Mr James started cutting down on his theatre time. I know Alex did the last operation and I think he's got a bit of a soft spot for Sammy.'

'It sounds as if you all do,' Jack said. 'I look forward to meeting him. He sounds a real character.'

'The ward certainly livens up when he's here,' Annie said wryly. 'He can't get about easily unless someone's available to lift him out of bed and into his chair so he ends up with the rest of the world coming to him, as though he were some Eastern potentate. You'll find there isn't an ounce of self-pity in him and he's a real tonic to have around.'

'Unlike Kevin,' Julie Thomas muttered darkly. 'Some patients really make your heart sink, don't they?'

'What's the matter with Kevin? He's only been here a couple of days and he seemed perfectly all right when he first came in.' Lauren was surprised to hear the young staff nurse's comment.

'He's always moaning about something,' she explained unhappily. 'I know he must be uncomfortable, having an operation down there, but... I don't know. Perhaps it's my fault.'

'What did he have done?' Jack prompted.

'Undescended testes,' Lauren supplied, having been in Theatre when the operation had been done. 'Completely straightforward. No complications, as far as I'm aware.'

'So what's his problem?' Jack turned back to Julie.

'He started off all right when he came back up to the ward after surgery. There was hardly a peep out of him except to ask for an extra pillow.'

She turned to Annie. 'You remember? I had to get a couple from stores because we'd already got several on the ward who were using extras and all the spares were in use.'

'What happened then?' Jack brought the conversation back to the original topic.

'Well, nothing really,' Julie said with a frown. 'He said his throat was a bit sore and he was sneezing a bit so I wondered at first if he might be coming down with a cold.'

'He didn't pull his stitches, sneezing, did he?'

'I don't think so because when I checked whether he was in any pain he said everything was all right…except for all these other niggles.'

'Is he still sneezing?'

'Yes, but he sounds almost as if he's getting over a heavy cold when he hasn't even had one. And he's gone all wheezy—almost as if he's asthmatic but the opposite way round, if you know what I mean.'

'You mean, he can't breathe in where an asthmatic can't breathe out?'

'That's right. And he's not joining in any of the things the rest of them are doing in the ward. He doesn't seem to be interested in the television or the computer games. Most of the time he's just curled up on his bed, looking miserable.'

There were several moments of silence while

everyone thought about the youngster, but no one had any flashes of inspiration.

'I'll make a point of having a chat with him and see if I can find out anything helpful,' Jack suggested. 'I hate to see any child miserable in hospital, even though they've usually come here to have something unpleasant done to them.'

Breakfasts had all been cleared away, and Julie regaled them with the tale of two of the children scheduled for surgery that morning, trying to sneak out to the kitchenette to get something to eat while no one was looking.

'How can you get them to understand that their hunger is less important than the risk of dying if you vomit under anaesthetic?' Annie exclaimed through her chuckles. 'We thought we'd cracked it, by getting them all to have their breakfasts in bed so we could keep a check on them, but these two obviously found the flaw in the system—they claimed they needed the bathroom.'

'Well, it all goes to prove that in a children's ward you have to be a mixture of nurse, mother and policeman or you don't stand a chance,' Lauren said with a laugh. 'I admire the way you cope with so many of them all at once. Jack and I have it easy. We only have to cope with them one at a time...usually when they're unconscious.'

'Speaking of unconscious children, it's about time we started some of these on their way,' Annie said with a glance at the watch pinned to the front of her dark blue uniform. She pushed herself swiftly to her feet and reached out to collect the empty mugs. 'If we don't give them their pre-meds in time, you're going to end up with a problem when they reach your end of the pipeline.'

As they all got ready to go their different ways Lauren realised that she'd enjoyed their little interlude so much that she was loath to leave. It had been so nice to talk to Jack, even within a group of people, that it had revived the memories of happier times.

Her more prudent side warned her that it would be far safer if she didn't tempt fate.

When Jack left the room and made his way down the ward towards the first of the children he was due to operate on Lauren watched him for a moment, unable to prevent herself from admiring everything about him. He wasn't only a handsome, virile man but as a doctor he was skilful and conscientious.

She watched the way he greeted the parents, sitting beside his first little patient, and saw that he possessed an empathy that enabled him to respond to the needs of his patients and their worried parents.

'Besotted,' she hissed in disgust, finally admitting that her attraction towards him was as strong as ever.

As if he'd heard her, he turned and glanced back in her direction. His eyes met hers for several long seconds, apparently without a trace of animosity in their depths, and her heart seemed to leap up into her throat.

Half of her wanted to spend more time with him and was tempted to go over to join him while he discussed the case, but the other, eminently sensible side recognised that there was such a legacy of unhappiness between them that 'little and often' was probably safer.

With an armful of papers and a look of concentration on her face, as if she had weighty matters on her mind, she took advantage of the fact that he was once more talking to the patient's parents to escape to the other end of the department to check up on Holly.

'She's not been doing so well,' Sunila reported with a worried frown.

'What's the matter with her?' Lauren's concern wasn't feigned. There was something about this baby girl which had called to her right from the first moment she'd seen her.

'Nothing major, if you look at all the monitors and the results of her tests, but…' She shook her head and gave a slight shrug.

'You mean you can't put your finger on it but you've got a feeling about her?' Lauren asked.

'Does that sound silly?' the younger woman asked. 'I know it isn't scientific.'

'A lot of what works isn't scientific—like cuddling and talking to the babies even when we know they can't possibly understand what we're saying—but we know it works because it happens time after time,' Lauren pointed out.

'Well, that's what it's like,' Sunila agreed. 'Her temperature's been up and down, but only very slightly, and we expect that with these tiny ones. As for the rest, all her levels are within normal ranges, but…' She pulled a face and shrugged again. 'I can't explain it.'

Lauren knew what she meant—she'd had those sorts of feelings about patients before—but she'd really thought that Holly was going to beat the odds.

'All we need is for her to get just a little bit stronger and she'll stand a better chance with the surgery,' she said in frustration. 'Has Noah been in to see her?'

'He's going to come in later on this morning,'

Sunila said. 'I thought of asking him to come in earlier—before lunch, perhaps—but there isn't really anything concrete to tell him. Nothing urgent enough to drag him away from what he's doing. It's not as if she's having breathing difficulties in the first stages of heart failure or anything.'

Lauren reached out a gentle finger and stroked the silky down just over Holly's tiny ear. She was just so small and fragile, so precious.

Lauren forced herself to step back and look around the unit. They were *all* precious, and it wouldn't do any of them much good if she was so focused on one child that the rest of them lacked attention.

The unit was a surprisingly busy place, with each baby requiring so much painstaking care and supervision that the ratio of staff to patients was high. There was a constant background noise from all the machinery, but when monitors were signalling problems the levels could rise enough to cause some babies unacceptable levels of stress.

The department had experimented with different regimens over the past few years and had found that if the day was interspersed with special 'quiet' times, when the lighting was reduced and soft, rhythmic sounds were played, it actually seemed to help their tiny charges.

'You've had a new one in,' Lauren exclaimed when, for the first time, she noticed that the humidicrib at the end was occupied. There was a whole array of monitors surrounding it, each one blinking and peeping as the nurse specialling the tiny occupant leaned over to adjust something.

'That's Karl. He came in late last night,' Sunila

said, her expression grim. 'His mother is...was...a German tourist.'

'Was?' Lauren questioned the change of tense with a sinking feeling. 'What happened?'

'They're not quite certain. One theory is that she forgot where she was and didn't look the right way when she stepped off the kerb. She was hit by a car, thrown up in the air and landed under the wheels of a bus.'

'Dear God,' Lauren breathed, horrified by the mental images. 'And her baby survived that?'

'Only because the paramedics who were first on the scene kept her going until they could get her to the hospital.'

'She didn't die instantly?' said Lauren.

'Apparently she was conscious just long enough to say something about the baby—they thought she was asking them to save her baby. Anyway, by the time they got her to St Augustine's she was already deeply unconscious from the head trauma and a couple of hours later she died.'

'But at least we managed to save her baby,' Lauren murmured, her heart clenching with pity for the motherless child. 'Do we know how premature he is?'

'More than a month but less than two is the estimate so far. They're hoping that someone will report his mother missing and we'll be able to find out more. She didn't have any rings on so they don't even know whether they're looking for a husband or what.'

Lauren shook her head, unable to imagine what it would be like to lose someone that way.

Suddenly her mind made one of those strange sideways leaps, and she found she *could* conceive what it would have been like. All she had to do was imagine how she would have felt if, after Jack had disappeared from their flat, the next thing she'd heard about him was that he'd been killed.

'Lauren? Are you all right?' Sunila asked in a worried voice. 'You've gone very white.'

'Have I?' she said faintly as she tried to banish her dreadful imaginings. 'I was just thinking how awful it would be if she was married...for her poor husband to find out...' She shook her head.

'Well, at the moment her little boy seems to be holding his own. There wasn't time to use steroids to give his lungs a better chance but he's not doing too badly.'

Lauren took one last look at Holly then turned to make her way across to the newest occupant of the unit.

'Oh, Lauren,' Sunila called quietly. 'Because his mother died there was no one to tell us what his name was so we thought... Well, the paramedic's name was Charles so we put the German form, Karl, on his file. Was that all right?'

'Well, it will certainly do until we can track down another member of his family,' Lauren agreed, feeling her throat tighten with the poignancy of the situation. 'He's too young to know any different if they want to change it.'

Lauren had to turn away quickly so that Sunila couldn't see her face. Sometimes memories surfaced and attacked her without warning, as they had just seconds ago.

All Sunila had done was tell her that little Karl had been given a name by the people who were caring for him so that he wouldn't be nameless.

She could never know for certain, but she had a terrible feeling that her own child hadn't fared as well.

Not that her parents had ever told her anything—in fact, they had refused even to discuss it, as if that whole episode in her life had never happened.

Suddenly she knew that she needed to be on her own for a moment, and she changed direction to walk across to the little interview room.

As she pulled the door closed behind her she was fighting for control and drew in a shuddering breath as a deep sob tried to force its way up.

It didn't matter how firmly she wanted to squash it back into the past, the memory loomed over her and once again she was waking up in a room she'd never seen before.

She'd felt so disorientated, her mouth as dry as though she'd been eating cotton wool and her head thumping almost as though she'd had too much to drink.

It had taken several minutes before she'd realised where she was—in a private room in the hospital her parents had chosen for her baby's delivery—and several more before she'd been able to summon the strength to reach for the bell.

Instead of the nurse she'd expected it had been the doctor she'd last seen in the delivery room who'd arrived at the door in answer to her summons.

He'd come in and closed it behind him before he turned to meet her gaze, and he'd been all wary eyes and careful smiles as he'd asked her how she was feeling.

Lauren remembered answering distractedly, but there had been only one thing she'd been interested in.

The last thing she remembered was the doctor telling her there was a problem and a mask being held over her face. There'd been too little time to ask questions, especially when she'd felt the searing bite of the hurriedly administered injection that had ushered in unconsciousness.

'I can't wait to hold my baby,' she exclaimed as her excitement finally vanquished the awful fuzzy feeling that plagued her. 'I know I've been asleep since the birth but I feel as if I've been waiting for ever.'

'Oh, but... My dear, your baby's gone,' he said bluntly. 'Didn't one of the nurses tell you?'

'Gone?' she repeated in horror, sick disbelief making her voice shrill as she struggled to sit up. 'What do you mean—gone? Gone where? What have you done with my baby?'

He looked distinctly uncomfortable and his eyes strayed towards the door as though he were looking for an escape route when she began again, terror lending a touch of hysteria to her tone.

'I want to see my baby,' she demanded. 'Tell someone to bring him...her... God, I don't even know which I had!' she cried, reaching out suddenly and catching hold of his arm, her nails digging into the sleeve of his suit.

'Tell me,' she shrieked, shaking his arm while tears of anguish streamed down her face. 'Tell me where my baby is. Let me see my baby.'

'My dear, that's not possible,' he said firmly, trying to peel her fingers off his arm. 'I told you there were...complications. You've been unconscious for nearly two days and—'

'Two days?' she repeated in disbelief, stunned that so much time had passed. 'Two days…'

Suddenly the anger drained out of her, as if someone had pulled a plug, and this time she made no attempt to hold onto him when he peeled her fingers off his arm.

As if from a long distance, she remembered watching the way he brushed the expensive fabric smooth again while the words 'two days' were echoing over and over inside her head.

She knew then that she wasn't ever going to be able to see her baby. If it had been born two days earlier, the body would have already gone for a post-mortem examination to confirm the cause of death, and after that…

She sank back against her pillows, every ounce of strength gone as she stared up at him and decided that she hated his smug, round, sweaty face and never wanted to see it again.

'How soon can I get out of here?' she demanded, with a lightning-fast glance around the fussy room and the sudden knowledge that she couldn't bear to stay one second longer than necessary.

'Well, my dear, it's only two days since…er… You've only been here two days and we recommend that our clients stay for at least a week and preferably ten days, just to make sure that their recovery is—'

'I *bet* you do,' Lauren said bitterly, suddenly having a good idea how he paid for his expensive suits and acquired the extra stones of weight stuffed inside them. 'Well, I'm afraid you're going to have to miss out on an extortionately padded bill this time because I'm leaving now.'

'Now? You want to leave now?' he gasped, standing there, gobbling like a turkey cock, while his face turned purple. 'But you *can't*. Your father said you were to stay here for at least—'

'It may have escaped your notice,' she broke in harshly, her voice grating over his and silencing him in mid-flow, 'but as I'm well over eighteen I neither need my father's nor your permission to leave if I want to. Now, please send someone in with my clothes or I'll walk out of the door as I am.'

Something in her expression must have told him she meant what she said but there was something in his eyes that she didn't trust.

Instinct told her that as soon as he was out of her sight he would be contacting her parents so she took the precaution of using the room's private telephone line to order a taxi straight away.

When her clothing arrived she ignored the dreadful shaking that seemed to have taken hold of every limb and was dressed and out of the door within minutes.

A grim smile pulled at the corners of her mouth when she recognised her father's car, hurriedly turning into the driveway as the anonymous taxi took her in the opposite direction. She had every intention of phoning home to let her parents know that she was all right, but just at that moment she'd had too much to come to terms with to bear their brand of smothering concern.

'I never even had a chance to say goodbye,' she whispered, the words sounding terribly loud in the little interview room as she scrubbed the tears away from her face.

Oh, she'd finally persuaded her father to find out the sex of the child but that was scant consolation.

'I never saw her, never held her…'

It was something that would haunt her for the rest of her life, the fact that her child had died and she'd never had the chance to tell her how much she was loved...

'Lauren?'

The voice behind her was the last one she wanted to hear while she was in this sort of state, but there was nothing she could do about it.

'Yes?' She kept her back to the door while she fumbled for her handkerchief and tried to scrub away the evidence of her tears.

It wasn't often that she lost control like this, and it had never happened at the hospital before. It must be because Jack was here as a visible reminder of all the heartache, pulling the memories that much closer to the surface.

'Is something wrong?' Jack asked, his voice closer now.

'No. No problem,' she said, with an attempt at non-chalance that was doomed to failure. 'It's just... sometimes it gets to me.'

'What?' he prompted quietly, this time from right behind her.

She closed her eyes and drew in a shuddering breath for control, only to smell the indefinable mixture of soap and man and medicine that had always meant Jack to her.

The urge to turn and bury herself in his arms was so strong that it nearly overcame her. Just at the last moment a ghostly echo of the memories she'd so recently relived rose up to remind her that when she'd needed him most Jack hadn't been around.

She'd had to survive without emotional help before

and she could do it again, even if it meant swallowing the accusations that hovered on the end of her tongue.

'They're so vulnerable,' she whispered, silently adding her little daughter…*their* little daughter…to the tally. 'There are so many unwanted babies in the world who thrive in spite of their parents, but when you see those little scraps…' she indicated the unit with a gesture '…fighting for their lives against such terrible odds… Sometimes it seems insurmountable.'

In the silence that followed her words she waited for him to say something—anything—and couldn't have been more shocked when, without a word, he pulled her firmly into his arms and cradled her head on his shoulder.

For long breathless moments all she was aware of was the warmth and strength of his embrace and the steady beat of his heart under her ear as she absorbed his comfort through every pore.

After the explosion of anger between them yesterday she would never have expected him to offer such sweet solace, even though he'd been perfectly civil to her today.

The trouble was that *this* Jack was the one she remembered from five years ago, the one she'd fallen in love with and cried bitter tears for when he was no longer in her life.

'I'd forgotten how soft you are, inside and out,' he murmured, his voice a deep rumble under her ear where it was pressed against his chest, and her own heart gave a silly leap at the remembered sound.

How many times had she gone to sleep with her head resting just here, his arms wrapped around her as if, even in sleep, he wanted to keep her close?

But, then, things hadn't been all they'd seemed. Far

from wanting to keep her close, he'd changed his mind about wanting her at all and hadn't even thought it important enough to tell her why.

That was what had grated on her all these years, she suddenly realised. *That* was what had robbed her of the confidence to search him out and demand an answer so that she could get on with her life with a new belief in herself.

If he hadn't destroyed her sense of self-worth perhaps she'd even have been strong enough to resist the pressure that had led to her disastrous marriage to Adrian...

'Jack...tell me why,' she whispered, almost before she knew she was going to say it, knowing that it was finally time to confront the truth.

'Why what?'

He loosened his hold slightly but she was too scared of what she might see in his face to take advantage and look up at him. It would be bad enough, just hearing the words.

'Why you had to do it like that...just pack up and leave without a word?'

CHAPTER SEVEN

'WHAT do you mean—when I left you?' Jack challenged in a voice full of surprise, his dark brows drawn sharply together. '*You* were the one who left *me*! When I got back you'd completely disappeared!'

'When you got back!' Lauren said scornfully, stepping back sharply so that all physical connection between them was broken. 'You make it sound as if you'd just popped out to buy a pint of milk.'

'But—'

'You were away for *days* before I realised you didn't intend coming back,' she continued, not allowing him the chance to interrupt. 'I thought I meant a little more to you than that. Do you know how it made me feel that you didn't even care enough to tell me it was over?'

'I left you a note,' he broke in furiously, his hand slashing through the air as though to cut his way through her diatribe. 'I told you why I had to go away. Surely you could have understood that…'

'Oh, yes. I understood,' she cut in, five years of bitterness behind the words. 'I needed you to be there for me but you were more interested in your own… *What* note?' His words suddenly registered. 'I left you a letter on the table and when I came back it had gone and so were you. There was no note from you. Not then and not later. Nothing.'

Anger and pain had tightened a band around her so

that it was lack of breath that finally stopped her words.

In the vibrating silence they suddenly heard an insistent knocking at the door and turned simultaneously towards it.

'Come.'

'Come in.'

They spoke at the same time, but with the anger swirling around them that was the only thing they were likely to do together in the foreseeable future.

'Sorry to intrude,' Julia Somerset said as she whisked briskly into the room and closed the door firmly behind her. 'But I thought you ought to know that your voices were loud enough to be heard right through the unit.'

Lauren was appalled.

How utterly unprofessional of them.

If it wasn't bad enough for them to have had an argument at the tops of their voices, they'd had it where everyone could hear their private business.

'Luckily, no one was down this end of the unit so no one heard what it was all about,' Julia continued, with more than a hint of censure in her voice. 'Even right outside the door things were pretty muffled. All I can say is if the two of you have unfinished business to settle from when you knew each other before then do it on your own time and do it quickly—for the sake of the department.'

With a brisk rustle of her uniform skirts the irate ward sister turned on her heel and before either of them could say a word she was gone.

'Ouch!' Jack muttered, and when Lauren chanced a glance at him she saw that his face was as red as hers felt.

'I think we'd do well to take her advice,' Lauren murmured, wondering sadly how everything had got so out of hand. 'We can't go on like this indefinitely.'

Jack agreed, but when it came to the matter of arranging a time to thrash everything out the only thing they could agree on was that it would have to happen somewhere away from the hospital.

'Luckily, Julia's discreet, but there are any number of staff who would delight in spreading gossip,' Lauren pointed out, concern for both their reputations clear in her mind.

'The dreaded hospital grapevine.' Jack pulled a face, his eyes filled with shadows as evidence of his turbulent thoughts. 'I suppose the only thing we can do in the meantime is behave as politely as if we're strangers who've only just met.'

Lauren didn't know if that was possible when every time she saw him she was assailed by memories of their time together, but for the sake of harmony she smiled her agreement.

It might be days before she got the answers to her questions the way their timetables were fixed at the moment, and Jack's reaction to the very first one told her that things might not be quite as clear-cut as she'd always thought.

Until then…

Until then they had plenty of work to do—work they both loved—and if they concentrated their energies on that, it could only be for the best.

They emerged into the unit and, by unspoken agreement, turned in opposite directions once they reached the corridor.

Lauren went back to her tiny babies to have her

first good look at Karl and was delighted by what she found.

'He's picked up such a lot since he first came up here,' she commented as she read the notes on his chart.

'He's a little sweetheart,' confirmed his carer with clear partisanship. 'He's ever so patient when I have to do anything for him and I'm sure he likes the sound of my voice when I'm talking to him.'

'From what I can tell, it won't be long before he can leave us for less specialised care,' Lauren confirmed when she'd finished her own evaluation. 'I know he was rushed in to us because no one knew what sort of state he was going to be in...'

'Well, he could have suffered injuries in the accident or he could have been very premature and had drastic breathing problems,' Day agreed, her knowledge of the possibilities gained through practical experience as well as training. 'It made sense to send him to us until we knew where we were with him.'

Her wide smile as she looked down at her little charge proved that her parents had known what they were doing when they'd named her 'Daylight'. Lauren had never known a nurse with such a wonderful gift for looking on the bright side of life.

'Now all we have to do is keep our fingers crossed that the police manage to track down some relatives,' Lauren said. 'It would be terrible if he'd survived such a tragedy only to end up unwanted and unloved.'

'He'll be all right,' Day declared confidently. 'I've got a feeling about him that everything's going to be just right.'

Lauren hoped she was right and found herself wishing that *she* had such boundless faith that things would turn out for the best.

Most of the time she had the belief in herself and what she did to know that her patients would benefit from her care, but it was her private life that seemed to lurch from one disaster to the next.

She remembered that thought about an hour later when she was called to the phone to take a call from her mother.

'It's not really convenient to talk now,' she remonstrated, embarrassed that the call had been switched through to a room full of colleagues. It was all very well that they had all looked away to give her a semblance of privacy, but that wouldn't stop their ears from working.

'Well, it's easier for me to call you at the hospital because I know you spend so much time there,' her mother countered, her carefully modulated voice slightly brusque. 'I wasn't certain that you'd get a letter and I wanted to make sure you got the invitation in time.'

'Invitation?' Lauren repeated faintly, already guessing what was coming with a sense of dread.

Her mother had organised some sort of social event and wanted her daughter to attend so she could introduce her to yet another in the unending parade of suitable partners.

'It's just a little party, cocktails and so forth…'

'Mother—' She might as well not have spoken.

'You'll need to be here before seven on Saturday but if you can get here on Friday so much the better. I can probably persuade Colin to do something with your hair at the same time he's doing mine—'

'Mother. I can't—'

As impervious to dissent as a Centurion tank, her mother ploughed on. 'I suppose there *are* some shops around there where you can buy yourself a new dress. It's not the same as a designer original but at least it'll be something new, and you want to make a good impression—'

'No,' Lauren said bluntly, deciding to opt for shock tactics.

It worked.

'Pardon, dear?' her mother said, her chilly tone indicating her affront at a refusal while trying to work out exactly what her daughter had refused—the hairdressing appointment, the shopping, the good impression...

'No, I won't be able to attend your little party,' Lauren clarified swiftly before her mother could start again. 'I'll be working.'

'Oh, but that's nonsense, dear. You're only a *junior* doctor, after all. They can quite easily do without you for the weekend, especially if you explain that I've gone to all this trouble to arrange—'

'That's not how the system works, Mother,' she said through gritted teeth, sheer exasperation at this oft-repeated argument forcing her to continue far more bluntly than she would have liked, especially with an audience. 'I'm sorry I haven't got time to discuss it, Mother, but I won't be able to come to your little do because I'll be on duty. I'll phone you.'

The Centurion tank was already revving into high gear again as she replaced the receiver as gently as if she expected it to explode in her hand. She drew in a deep breath before she turned back to face her colleagues.

Sunila met her gaze with a sympathetic grimace.

'I've had phone calls like that from *my* mother,' she said wryly. 'It usually means that she's lined up yet another son of yet another one of her friends for me to meet. She's very proud of my work but she knows I'm meeting people all day and she's afraid I'll want to marry one of them. She's absolutely determined I'm going to marry someone with strong roots to the old country.'

'That only goes to prove that mothers are the same all over the world,' Lauren commented, relieved that at least one of her colleagues knew what she was going through. 'I'll probably get a phone call from my father next, demanding that I apologise for upsetting all Mother's plans.'

'The only solution I've found is to offer an alternative. You know. "I can't come this weekend but I should be able to visit next Sunday." Something like that.'

'And with *next* Sunday being Mothering Sunday, you might even score a few extra points,' Julia pointed out. 'You could even take her some flowers or chocolates to help mend fences.'

'I don't like to give her too much warning or there's no knowing what arrangements I'll walk into. It's a bit like negotiating a minefield,' Lauren admitted with unusual candour.

There was an empty ache inside her for all the things that were missing in her life and it seemed to loosen her tongue.

'You're lucky yours value your career. Mine seem to view it as something to do to fill in time before I marry and have a family, and just recently I think they've decided it's time I did something about presenting them with a grandson. Of course, I'm expected just to fall in with their plans.' She groaned her frustration, refusing to think about the pain of lost chances.

'If there was any other way of satisfying their dynastic desires I'd jump at the chance, but I object to the idea of being matched by bloodlines, like some brood mare.'

If Lauren hadn't been watching Jack's face as she spoke she'd never have seen the way his expression changed in the space of just a few words.

Until that moment he'd been idly following the conversation between the three women with typical male detachment.

The look on his face was anything but detached now. For a second he glared at her but then his eyes were filled with something almost like fear before he suddenly got to his feet and strode out of the room.

Virtually simultaneously the phone rang. It was Annie, wanting to know where to reach Jack.

'He was here a moment ago but left in a hurry,' Lauren told her. Sunila went to the door to try to catch him but shook her head. 'Sorry, he's gone. Is it anything I can help with?'

'I don't know. His mother's here and was hoping to have a word with him about Danny.'

'He might be on his way to you,' Lauren suggested, without any real idea of what had sent him hurrying out of the room or where he was going. 'If he doesn't arrive in the next few minutes, give me a call and I'll come and see if I can help.'

With possibilities creating a traffic jam inside her head, Lauren made her way towards the other end of the department and her precious babies. She wanted to spend just a few minutes with them before she had to attend to the afternoon's paediatrics intake.

'How is everyone doing?' she asked Julia as she entered the unit, her eyes automatically gravitating towards Holly's cot.

'It's Leonie who's been keeping us on the hop today,' she said, clearly concerned.

'Leonie?' Lauren frowned and glanced around. 'Which one is she?'

'The surviving twin,' Julia said, and gestured in her direction. 'Her mother visited her for the first time about an hour ago and told us her name. They'd been going to call the little boy Leo, but when he died they made the name a mixture of the two so they didn't lose him completely.'

'What's been the matter with her?' Lauren asked, getting back to the original topic of conversation.

'I'm not certain but it's almost as if her controls have gone haywire. Her heart rhythm's all over the place as well as her breathing—when she remembers to do it. I don't think we've had a single normal result from her in hours.'

'Isn't the positive pressure helping her breathing?' Lauren asked, worried about the significance. She knew that the effect of pressure on the oxygen supply should be enough to trigger the breathing reflex. If it wasn't working it could either mean that the pressure needed to be raised or...or perhaps the poor little scrap had already suffered brain damage so that she *couldn't* respond.

'It's helping...more or less but... I don't know, it sounds stupid but it's almost as though she's...as though she's restless or something.'

Julia's words sparked a distant memory. Lauren

stood still and concentrated for a moment and suddenly it came into focus.

'This might sound completely off the wall,' she began hesitantly. 'I read something about it in a journal...just a theory...but do you think she could be missing her twin?'

There was startled silence for a moment while Julia absorbed the suggestion, but then she grinned.

'You never know,' she said. 'But it's certainly worth seeing what we can do to stop her feeling lonely if that's what the problem is.'

There was nothing else Lauren could think of to suggest at the moment, and it was time for her to hurry through to the other end of the department to check today's intake of new patients and get all their tests started so that everything would be ready for the morning.

It was a very long, very busy afternoon, filled with fractious children and worried parents.

Jilly was a five-year-old girl who was coming in to have plastic surgery to flatten her ears. The poor little thing had already had her first term at school ruined by taunts of 'Dumbo' and 'jug handles', but with the best will in the world Lauren had to admit that she'd rarely seen ears that stuck out more.

At least Lauren could reassure her that the discomfort of the operation would be a once-in-a-lifetime thing that would transform her appearance for ever.

The second admission was a six-year-old boy, arriving preparatory to having kidney stones removed.

Unfortunately, his parents had been forced to bring his younger brothers with them, and Lauren realised very quickly that there was going to be a problem.

Young Damien was very pale and quiet and, just

from the expression in his eyes, she could tell that he was very frightened about what was going to happen to him.

It was sad to see him bravely trying to help his mother keep his boisterous brothers under control while what he really needed was her undivided attention.

Lauren made a note in the file to come back later when the younger siblings had gone home to bed. Perhaps, when everything was quieter, she would be able to talk to him and find out what he was worried about. He needed to have his mind put at rest before he went down for the operation.

The third admission was Sammy Tolliver, and as soon as he appeared on the ward in his diminutive powered wheelchair the atmosphere changed.

'Perhaps all I need to do is put him next to Damien,' Lauren murmured, wondering if the young live-wire would help to cheer the other child up.

She thought about it for a moment then realised that it was probably the last thing the much quieter boy wanted. He already had more competition than he needed at home from two younger brothers. The least she could do was make his stay in hospital as stress-free as possible.

She glanced across at Danny and when she saw that the bed next to his was still empty she resolved to suggest the allocation to Annie.

She didn't know either child well, and Danny was due to go home in a day or two, but he would definitely be a more peaceful neighbour for Damien than Sammy.

By the time everything had been organised to her satisfaction she was relieved to see Damien's siblings on their way out of the ward with their father. With only his mother beside him she decided it was probably the best chance she was going to get to speak to them.

'The others have gone off, exploring, have they?' she asked as she joined them.

'They were getting a bit bored so their dad's taken them to the hospital cafeteria for a snack,' Damien's mother explained, and Lauren suddenly noticed the lines of stress bracketing her mouth and eyes.

'It can be very upsetting for the whole family the first time one of them has to come into hospital,' Lauren said, giving her an opening if she wanted to talk.

With a tired smile she took the opportunity gratefully. 'It wouldn't be so bad if we knew what was going to happen to him,' she said. 'We haven't really got anyone we can leave the other two with and we haven't liked to ask too many details while they're there, listening.'

'Well, you wouldn't want to make them jealous, would you?' Lauren suggested outrageously, with a hidden wink for the mother.

Damien didn't look as if he believed what he was hearing.

'Why would they be jealous? I've got to have an operation.'

'Ah, but what *they* don't know is that you're going to have a special machine used on you,' Lauren continued. 'It was developed from research into why the canopies of jet aeroplanes shattered when it rained.'

Damien was enthralled as she told the story of researchers, finding out that at certain speeds the raindrops produced sound waves that damaged the cockpit canopies.

When she went on to explain how special equipment would focus similar shock waves on the kidney stones to shatter them into dust she could see that he was utterly enthralled.

By the time the rest of the family returned his only concern was the fact that he would have to be asleep for the whole procedure and would miss seeing it happen.

As she walked away from Damien's family she noticed that the influx of early evening visitors had started and only then realised how much time had passed.

In the next bed she saw that Danny's grandmother was quietly sharing a storybook with him, and suddenly remembered that she had been trying to get in contact with Jack.

'Hello, Doctor,' piped Danny when he saw her approaching his bed. 'I've been practising the secret and it's been working every time.'

'Well done,' she praised, almost as pleased as if he were her own child.

His ruffled hair tempted her to smooth her hand over the dark spikes, but she suddenly remembered her quest and turned her attention to the older woman seated beside his bed.

'Mrs Madison? Did you manage to get in contact with Jack earlier?' she asked, feeling rather guilty that she hadn't checked up sooner.

'Hello, Doctor.' She smiled, obviously recognising Lauren from the night before. 'He sent a message to say that he'd come along as soon as he could, but I haven't seen him yet.'

'Was it anything that I can help you with—something in the medical line—or did you just want to have a private word with him?'

'A bit of each really,' she admitted. 'I wanted to know how Danny's doing and when he'll be well enough to come home, and I needed to know what Jack's shifts were over the next few days so that I can organise some appointments. I don't drive myself, and it either means getting Jack to drive me or getting a taxi.'

'Well, I might be able to help you with both problems,' Lauren volunteered. 'I can tell you that we're very pleased with Danny's progress. He's recovering beautifully and we don't anticipate any problems. At this rate he'll probably be back home with you in two or three days.'

'Oh, that *is* good news,' she said with a beam. 'The house has been so empty and quiet without him, especially with Jack spending the night at the hospital too.'

'I didn't realise he was on duty last night,' Lauren exclaimed in surprise. 'He'd been here all day as well.'

'Oh, he wasn't on duty. I think he just wanted to be here for Danny,' Mrs Madison confided.

'Well, I can't tell you offhand what his duties are—most of the time I can't remember my own, without looking at the timetable—but it won't take me long to find out.'

'Are you sure? I wouldn't want to put you to any trouble, especially for someone who's still very much a stranger to you.'

'Oh, Jack's not a stranger,' Lauren confessed, surprising herself when she suddenly realised just how much truth there was to her words. Right from the first time they'd met she'd felt as if there'd been a connection between them, almost as if they'd known each other before. 'I don't suppose he's had a chance to tell you, but we actually met about five years ago when we were training.'

An uncertain frown crept over the older woman's face and her eyes flicked once from Lauren's face to the name badge clipped to her top pocket.

'Dr L. Scott-Dakers?' she said questioningly. 'I'm sorry, I don't recognise the name but, then, I didn't see much of him when he was training so I probably wouldn't have heard of you.'

'Oh, you wouldn't recognise the name anyway,' she said, glad that Jack was unlikely to have mentioned her name to his mother. She liked the woman and was pleased that there was none of the tension between them that existed between herself and Jack.

'I suppose that's the curse women have to bear when they marry and change their names,' she continued with a chuckle. 'They can easily lose contact with people just because no one knows what name they're looking for. I was Lauren Hamilton before I married.'

She paused expectantly, waiting to see whether the name meant anything to Jack's mother, and was startled to see the colour drain out of her cheeks until she was quite grey.

'Mrs Madison? Are you feeling all right?'

For a moment Lauren was certain that the older woman was going to faint, but at the last moment she rallied and lifted her chin in a gesture so reminiscent of Jack that she suddenly realised where he'd learned it.

'I'm fine, Doctor,' she insisted staunchly, clasping the forgotten book to her like a shield. 'Absolutely fine. Don't you worry about me. I'll just wait here for Jack to come. If he said he'll be here soon then he'll be here. He was raised to keep his word and he's never let me down yet.'

Lauren felt her forehead pleat into a frown when she heard the strange emphasis Jack's mother was placing on her words, but when a repeated offer to look up his timetable was met with a firm refusal there was nothing else to keep her there.

'See you tomorrow, Danny,' she said with a smile, sorry not to have more of a chance to talk to him.

'See you,' he echoed with a brief wave, then added in a stage whisper, 'I'll remember our secret.'

His grandmother gave a strangled groan and when Lauren looked at her in concern she saw that, if anything, the woman was paler than ever.

'Are you sure I can't get you something?' Lauren offered again, worried that the woman was ill.

'Jack,' she gasped agitatedly. 'Just find Jack.'

Lauren hovered for a moment, but when her presence actually seemed to be increasing the woman's uneasiness she hurried off to track Jack down.

Not wanting to cause Mrs Madison any further upset, Lauren sent Annie over a few minutes later with the message that Jack would be there in about a quarter of an hour. However, her concern wouldn't let her turn her back and walk away so she walked across to Kevin's bed and perched herself on the edge for a chat.

The fact that she was able to keep an eye on Danny and his grandmother started off being the primary reason she'd positioned herself there, but when she tried to start a conversation with the withdrawn youngster gradually her attention was caught by his obvious misery.

'When can I go home?' he wheezed, clearly close to tears.

'It'll be a couple of days yet,' Lauren had to tell him, sorry that he was so unhappy. 'We have to make sure that the operation's worked properly or you'll only have to come in again.'

'I wouldn't,' he said with the first show of determination she'd seen from him yet. 'I'm not *ever* coming back here, not even if all my insides fall out on the floor.'

Lauren blinked at his vehemence, fighting a grin at the gruesome mental image he'd evoked.

'Has your stay here been so dreadful?' she asked gently. 'Most people find there's lots to do as soon as their operation is over and plenty of people to talk to.'

He stared up at her silently, the picture of stubbornness with his back turned to the rest of the room. For a while she thought he wasn't going to answer but decided it was important to wait him out. There were any number of studies that showed that an unhappy patient didn't heal as well or as fast as a happy one.

'I can't *breathe* properly in hospital,' he said suddenly, the words bursting out of him as if he couldn't contain them any more. 'There's something… something heavy on my chest and my head's all bunged up and…' He wheezed as he dragged in a breath and raised his hands in surrender.

'When did all this start?' Lauren questioned gently, full of sympathy for the unhappy boy but not sure she could do anything to help.

'After the operation,' he said sullenly. 'I was all right until I came back to this bed and now I'm getting worse and worse.'

'Does it help if you have a pile of pillows to prop you up?'

'That's what the nurse asked. She had to go away and get some more but they only seemed to make it worse…and they feel all funny too,' he added crossly.

'What do you mean—funny?' Lauren asked, temporarily sidetracked by his comment.

'They're not like my pillow at home. They're all…all squidgy, as if they've got slippery, prickly things inside,' he complained.

'What do you mean?' Lauren reached out to feel one of the mound of pillows surrounding the unhappy child and felt only the familiar resilience of synthetic stuffing.

'That one's all right. It's this one and this one that feel so funny,' he directed, prodding the two on top of the mound.

Lauren rubbed the filling of the pillow between her fingers and smiled when she realised that it felt exactly as Kevin had described it.

'It's filled with feathers,' she explained with a smile. 'Here, if you rub it you can feel the little spines of the feathers. Are the other ones like yours at home?'

'Yes. I can remember Mum saying to her friend that she could wash them in the machine and if they burst it doesn't go everywhere.'

'Do you and your brother use them to have pillow fights?' she asked, and was delighted by the way Kevin opened up to reveal how bright and intelligent he really was.

The germ of an idea had taken root in the back of her head, and the longer she talked to Kevin the more she wondered if there could be any truth to it.

'Have you got any pets at home, Kevin?' she prompted, testing her hypothesis.

'No, worse luck,' he groaned. 'I wanted to have a dog, or even a rabbit, but Dad says they spread hairs all round the place and it makes him sneeze.'

'Do they make you sneeze?'

'Dunno. I never had one.'

'What about birds? A budgerigar?'

'No. My gran used to have one, but he died and she didn't get another one.'

Lauren straightened purposefully, almost certain she knew what was wrong with Kevin. Out of the corner of her eye she caught sight of Jack, striding towards Danny's bed, but while her heart gave a strange lurch in her chest it was important that she tested her theory.

'Kevin, would you mind if I took the two slippery pillows away for a while, just to try something out?'

'I don't mind. Sometimes it's more comfortable to lie down so the stitches don't pinch me...' he glanced shyly towards his lap '...down there.'

Lauren piled the pillows in her arms and said her goodbyes before she carried them over to Annie.

'I'm hoping that I've solved young Kevin's problem,' she said, dumping her burden on the corner of the desk. 'I've got a feeling that he's allergic to feathers and that's what these are filled with.'

'Even if they are, it shouldn't be a problem because all the pillows are sealed in a plastic cover under the pillowcase,' Annie objected. 'It's done for hygiene reasons.'

'Well, I'm betting that there are some tiny holes in the plastic and they're letting out just enough fibres from the feathers to set off a reaction in Kevin,' Lauren announced with a satisfied smile. 'I reckon that if his bedding is changed to get rid of any traces then by morning he'll be a different lad altogether.'

'It's certainly worth a try,' Annie agreed. 'I'll get someone on it straight away.'

Lauren released a slightly weary breath and was just wondering whether there was anything else she ought to do before she went home when she was suddenly aware that someone had come up to stand behind her.

'I want a word with you,' growled Jack, right in her ear. 'What on earth did you say to upset my mother?'

Surprise made her whirl to face him, and the expression on his face was enough to blister the paint off the walls.

CHAPTER EIGHT

'I HAVEN'T said anything!' Lauren exclaimed indignantly. 'I sent a message for you to come straight away because she didn't look very well. I wondered if she'd been overdoing things with Danny, or if—'

'Don't give me that,' Jack snapped, completely dismissing her concerns. He glanced around quickly, and in view of their tongue-lashing earlier Lauren thought sourly that he was probably checking to see where Annie was before he continued.

'My mother's not so old or feeble that an hour or two sitting at a child's bedside will exhaust her when she's been taking full time child-minding in her stride for most of Danny's life.'

The sound of a childish tantrum at the other side of the room drew his attention for a second, breaking his concentration.

'This is hopeless,' he muttered in exasperation. 'I was going to take her home but this won't wait. I'll just go and tell her that I'll be a bit longer and then we'll find somewhere to talk.'

'Look, there's no point whatever in dragging me off somewhere and giving me the third degree. I'm afraid I've absolutely no idea what's going on. If she says I've upset her then I'm very sorry, but I don't know—'

'Dr Scott-Dakers?' called a voice, breaking into her low-voiced attempt at persuasion.

Lauren sighed, not certain whether she was pleased

or sorry for the interruption. It wasn't that she was particularly keen to talk to Jack when he was in such an abrasive mood, but if they didn't sort things out soon she was going to end up going mad.

'Yes, Sister Denton,' she replied over the hubbub of voices and television programmes.

'There's a telephone call for you. You can take it in my office.'

Lauren signalled her thanks and threaded her way through the toys that had gradually crept out across the floor from the play corner.

Once in the relative silence of Sister's office she picked up the phone.

'Dr Scott-Dakers,' she said, her thumb and forefinger rubbing the headache nagging at her temples.

She turned to lean wearily back against the desk, propped on the edge to take her weight off her feet while she waited for the call to be put through.

A sound in the room made her eyes fly open and she suddenly realised that Jack had followed her. He stood there, his feet planted solidly in the middle of the only free space in the room with a glower on his face.

'I said there was nothing to talk about,' she said angrily as she glared up at him, just as the click in her ear told her the line was open.

'I'll thank you to remember your manners, young lady,' snapped her father. 'If that's the way you spoke to your mother, it's no wonder she was so upset.'

'Damn,' she breathed, and squeezed her eyes tightly shut. 'Hello, Father. They didn't tell me it was you on the line.'

'Well, who did you think it would be after that disgraceful display of bad manners? Now, you'd better get yourself organised so that you get here on Friday evening or I'll want to know the reason why. Your mother's gone to a great deal of trouble over this event—not that you're ever likely to show any gratitude. She's invited dozens of people and the least you can do is make sure that…'

Years of practice had helped Lauren to switch off to the hurtful asides and concentrate on the main thread of any lecture from her father.

She didn't think they'd ever had a real conversation. It was usually this way… He told her what he expected her to do and she complied.

At least it always *had* been that way until four and a half years ago when she'd dared to defy him for the first time. Not that it had done her any good in the long run, as far as the baby's life was concerned.

The one thing that *was* different was the fact that she was more prepared to stand up to him these days.

She was counting to ten while she tried to find a new way of saying no when a sudden memory of what Sunila had said earlier in the day came back to her. Something about offering an alternative…?

Blunt refusal was a method that only brought hours of recrimination so perhaps it might be worth a try.

'I'm sorry, Father, but it's going to be completely impossible this weekend because I'm rostered to work,' she announced firmly. 'I thought you and Mother would be pleased if I came to visit on Mothering Sunday, but if that's not convenient…?'

There were several seconds of blessed silence following her interruption, as if he couldn't believe what he'd heard, and then she heard the sound of some hasty muttering in the background.

She heard her mother wail something about it being

too late to cancel the party now and that the only reason she'd organised it in the first place had been to introduce Lauren to Joan's nephew. Then she heard her grudging acceptance of the alternative.

'That sounds as if it will be all right,' her father announced briskly. 'Do you know what time you'll get here?'

'Can I let you know closer to the time?' Lauren temporised, amazed that the ploy actually seemed to be working. 'It will depend on whether there have been many emergencies how early I can get away—perhaps we'll be lucky and manage the whole weekend—but I'm already looking forward to that special meal Mother usually organises.'

'Yes. Well. We'll be hearing from you, then,' he replied, apparently at a loss once the direction of the conversation had been taken out of his hands.

Lauren put down the receiver with a sigh of relief and was startled to hear a slow handclap.

'You're a quick learner,' he said without a trace of a smile. 'Sunila only gave you the idea today and already you're an expert.'

'Beginner's luck's more like it,' she suggested with a nervous smile. 'It's never happened like that before so it took him by surprise.'

Jack didn't return the smile, his folded arms a symbolic fortification against her that told her he wasn't here to exchange pleasantries.

'You'd better let them know I kept my promise,' he said suddenly, his expression hard. 'I'll always be grateful to them so they need to know that it was sheer coincidence that put us together here. I didn't come looking for you.'

Lauren frowned as she tried to work out what he

was talking about. She knew that neither of them had ever expected to be working together again, and if he'd known her married name...

'What promise?' she demanded, ignoring the stab of pain that came with his confirmation that he hadn't wanted to see her again. 'Who did you make a promise to?'

'What promise?' he mimicked, and gave a sarcastic laugh. 'You *know* what promise. The promise I had to make to your parents.'

'My parents?' Lauren couldn't believe what she was hearing. 'But you never met my parents.'

'I didn't *need* to meet them to get the message. They passed it on loud and clear. Stay out of your life, or else.'

'Or else what?' Lauren demanded, feeling as if she were trapped in the middle of a nightmare with no way to wake up.

'There it is again—that injured, innocent look!' he exclaimed with false amazement, but his expression changed in the blink of an eye.

'Just you remember, Lauren,' he continued in a threatening growl. 'I kept my promise and now you've got to keep yours. I stayed out of your life because that was what *you* wanted. Well, the boot's on the other foot now. You can stay out of mine.'

Sheer amazement had taken the starch out of her knees and Lauren sank back onto the edge of the desk, quite certain that she couldn't have moved if she'd wanted to as she watched him stalk out of the room.

All the way home she worried at the conversation, like a terrier at a bone, turning it over and over.

When she should have been sorting laundry and

changing her sheets she found herself sitting with yet another cold cup of tea in her hand, her unopened post scattered on the carpet at her feet.

She'd remembered to feed Desperate Dan and Jack the Ripper... Well, she hadn't really had any option when they'd virtually mugged her as she came in the door.

Now they were sitting, watching her, as if they knew that there was something wrong, but she hardly noticed.

Her whole concentration was on the conversation today, and it didn't seem to matter how many different ways she played it over in her mind she was left with the same question.

What on earth *had* Jack been talking about?

As far as she knew, her parents had never even known of his existence. Well...in view of her pregnancy they'd known there'd been *someone*, but the only person Lauren had breathed his name to had been Adrian. He'd been her friend and neighbour ever since she could remember and they'd shared an alliance against over-zealous parents right through their childhood. He would *never* have told them anything she'd confided...

Her stomach took a sickening dive.

Suddenly she remembered the odd sideways looks she'd caught Adrian sharing with her parents, and she wasn't so certain any more.

Had he told her parents who had fathered her child?

If they *had* known about Jack, had they contacted him? Was this why he bore her so much animosity?

How could she find out?

Her heart clenched with sorrow when she realised

that her first thought had been to ask Adrian, but her best friend wasn't there any more.

Since his death it had been as if she'd lost a huge chunk of her past. There was no one else who would remember the madcap schemes he'd talked her into, or the way she'd had to practise thinking on her feet to get him out of the punishments they'd attracted.

Lauren sighed heavily when she remembered that there were still legalities to be sorted out after her old friend's death. In fact, she could see from here that one of the envelopes by her feet bore the embossed logo of the Scott-Dakers' family solicitors.

As far as she could gather, Adrian had left a package for his wife in their safekeeping. It was her feelings of guilt that wouldn't let her claim it...not when she'd never been able to allow herself to be a real wife to him.

How else was she going to find out about what happened five years ago?

Certainly not from Jack.

After his outburst this afternoon it seemed that he had some hidden agenda of his own and she would be the *last* person he'd talk to about it.

Adrian's parents weren't an option. Since the death of their son they'd hardly spoken to the Hamilton family, obviously blaming them for their loss. It was hard to remember how delighted they'd been that the two families had been united on the day she and Adrian had married...

The only other people she could ask were her parents.

She glanced across at the telephone then shook her head. This was a conversation she wanted to have face to face. As far as she knew, although she hadn't always agreed with what her parents had wanted for her, they had always been open and honest with her about their reasons.

They were both incurable snobs about their background but each gave generously of their time and money for those less fortunate than themselves. She was finding it difficult to imagine the two of them forcing Jack into some weird bargain to make him stay away from her.

'Now I wish I *was* going to that dratted party,' she groaned when she realised it was going to be a week until she saw them.

'Well, sitting here isn't going to get me any closer to an answer,' she grumbled, as she leant forward to scoop her shoes off the floor.

The logo on the solicitors' envelope taunted her as it lay there in the middle of the mess, and she snatched it up.

'All right! All right!' she snapped as she prised the flap open and drew out the single sheet of heavy stationery. 'I'm reading it, OK?'

The essence of the letter was basically the same as each of the ones they'd sent her since Adrian's death but the tone had gradually changed.

This one actually bore a hand-written postscript in which the elderly solicitor almost pleaded with her, for the sake of the grieving parents, to allow a final conclusion to the matter.

Lauren sat, clutching the letter, while the two cats tried to climb up on her lap, but she swatted them away absently. She didn't need a demanding distraction while she finally came to the realisation that *she* needed to find some sort of closure too.

With that admission came the determination to see

it through. If she was going to travel down to her parents' house for Mothering Sunday, maybe she could arrange to pick up this package at some point?

Perhaps then she'd be able to live with the guilt that hovered like a small dark cloud at the back of her mind.

'Good morning... Oh, it's only you,' said Sunila, obviously disappointed when she saw it was Lauren entering the unit the next morning.

'Well, I'm so sorry to disappoint you. Who were you expecting?'

'I don't know whether "expecting" is the right word. More like hoping, I think,' she said glumly. 'We've been trying to get in touch with Holly's parents for several hours now and haven't made contact yet.'

'Which parents?' Lauren looked round before she continued in a quieter voice. 'The surrogate parents who never wanted her in the first place or the parents who arranged for her to exist then rejected her when she wasn't perfect?'

'Not that you feel in the *least* bit emotional about the situation,' Sunila teased.

Lauren grimaced. 'You know you feel just as strongly about the situation,' she pointed out. 'I could, perhaps, understand it if this was happening in one of the countries where every visit to a doctor, every pill and every operation had to be paid for with cash. People *would* be terrified of taking on a child that's going to need major, extortionately expensive surgery. But in Britain, where she'll be able to have a life-saving operation whenever she needs it, without any of them having to put their hands into their pockets—'

'That's why we've been trying to get hold of them,'

Sunila interrupted. 'The "whenever" just moved a lot closer.'

'What?' Lauren's eyes focused instantly on the little scrap in the cot, her brain automatically registering her colour and respiration before she glanced over the monitor displays for the rest of the information. 'Did something happen during the night?'

'She's been fighting for breath. Noah had to come in and put her back on positive pressure and increase the concentration of oxygen, but the only thing that's going to do any permanent good is to do the operation.'

'When was he thinking of?' Lauren asked. 'Originally, he was hoping to wait until she was bigger and stronger.'

'Now he wants to do it as soon as he can get the permission signed,' Sunila said sombrely. 'That's why he's been trying to get hold of the parents.'

Lauren stood silently looking down at Holly, and saw the struggle she was having to get enough oxygen around her little body to keep everything functioning.

Every fibre in Lauren's body was straining with the urge to help Holly with the fight, her hands clenched into white-knuckled fists as she wondered, as ever, if *this* was what had killed her own daughter.

Suddenly aware that she'd been standing there far too long, she straightened away from the cot.

'I've got to go over to the other side now, but you will keep me posted, won't you?'

'Whatever happens,' Sunila promised. 'Hopefully, to tell you that the parents have been in to sign the permission.'

Neither of them mentioned the possibility that she

might have to contact Lauren to tell her that Holly had taken a turn for the worse.

There was chaos in the ward when Lauren arrived over the other side, with various people dashing in every direction.

Lauren knew that when several children had to be prepared for the morning surgery list things could get a bit fraught, but this was something else.

'What on earth's happening?' she asked Annie when she appeared round the corner, looking less than her immaculate self.

'Jilly's locked herself in the staff toilet,' she declared briefly. 'Her mother and father are trying to get her to unlock the door but she won't even talk to them.'

'Oh, Lord. And she was going to be first on the list because she seemed the most nervous.'

'Now we don't know what to do—hold up the list for her and make everyone else late or tack her onto the end and make her go through hours of waiting.'

'And you say she's not talking?' Lauren asked.

'Not a word.'

Lauren tried to think of a solution but she hadn't come across this situation before and was going to have to wing it.

'It would have to be the staff toilet,' she muttered, just in case one of the other children was listening to her conversation with Annie and got ideas. 'The rest have all got child-safety locks so we could have got her out.'

'Don't think I hadn't realised that,' Annie said darkly. 'As soon as this little fiasco is over I'm getting Maintenance up to change the lock!'

'In the meantime, shall I go to try and talk to her?'

'Please! And the best of luck.'

Lauren took Jilly's father aside for a moment and between them they tried to map out a strategy that wouldn't involve the additional trauma of breaking the door down.

'Jilly, can you hear me?' she called, not expecting an answer as she settled herself on the floor outside the door. 'My name's Lauren and I'm a doctor. You saw me yesterday afternoon when you came into hospital. Do you remember?'

There wasn't a sound from behind the door but Lauren had a feeling that Jilly was listening to everything that was going on.

'Your mummy and daddy are just going along the corridor to get a cup of coffee and they've asked me if I will keep you company so you don't get frightened all by yourself.'

There was a slight scuffling sound and Lauren permitted herself a little smile.

'It can be very frightening when you come to a strange place for the first time—like your first day at school. I bet that was a bit scary, especially when your mummy went home without you.'

This time she was certain she heard a little sob but she didn't dare to stop now.

'It's not like that here, you know, Jilly,' she said, leaning closer towards the door to make certain the frightened youngster heard every word. '*Here*, we know it's frightening so we make sure you can stay with your mummy and daddy all the way. And when you wake up after it's all over I promise you they'll still be right there beside you, holding your hand.'

Lauren paused, running out of words for a moment and trying to think what other nightmares might have prompted this cry for help. All she'd been able to think about was the fact that the poor child had just had a horrendous first term at school.

'Promise?' came a little whisper from the other side of the door, so quiet that Lauren almost missed it.

'What was that, sweetheart?' she prompted, dropping her own volume a little now that she knew Jilly was close by. 'What did you say?'

'Promise you won't make them go away,' she said, and Lauren had to swallow a lump in her throat when she heard how the little voice was shaking with fear.

'I promise,' Lauren said solemnly, then a flash of mischief took over. 'Or else you can paint my nose bright blue with purple dots.'

She waited with her fingers crossed and then she heard what she'd been listening for—a giggle.

'Is that a good enough promise for you to unlock the door?' Lauren asked, holding her breath that she hadn't pushed too quickly.

She caught sight of a movement out of the corner of her eye and turned to see Jack, leaning up against the wall, just a few feet away. How long had he been there? She'd been concentrating so hard that she hadn't even seen him arrive.

From her position on the floor he looked impossibly tall, all long lean legs and wide shoulders with the pale green theatre scrubs stretched across his broad chest by his folded arms.

It was obvious from his garb that he'd heard about the problem on the ward and had come to help, but what wasn't so obvious was what he was thinking while he watched her.

His blue-grey gaze was very intent as he looked

down at her and it made her feel almost as if he were seeing her with microscopic clarity.

The sound of the lock clicking open snapped her attention back to the problem at hand.

Much as she would have liked to have taken the time to analyse the expression on his face, Jilly was her concern now and she forced herself to shut him out of her mind as she waited for the door to open.

The little face that peered around the edge of the door was streaked with tears and, without having to think about it, Lauren opened her arms in invitation.

With a little sob Jilly launched herself at Lauren, nearly knocking her over, but that didn't stop her wrapping her arms securely around the little body.

'Shall we go and find your mummy and daddy?' she murmured into the sweat-dampened hair, and smiled at the fervent nod.

By the time Lauren had carried her to her waiting parents the maintenance man was already standing, waiting, with his toolbox.

'I'm not taking any more chances,' Annie declared. 'It only put us back twenty minutes this time, but if it happened again who knows? We're getting more and more day cases coming through, and until the specialist day unit is up and running that means we're going to be getting busier and busier on theatre days.'

Lauren was assisting that morning and the list was a mixture of tonsillectomies and hernia repairs but she did manage to arrange for a camera to be taken along to the special unit where the excorporeal shock-wave lithotripter would be used on Damien's kidney stones.

She hadn't told him what she'd intended in case nothing came of it, but the nurse who'd accompanied him on his journey had been primed to try to get some pictures of him in the complicated machinery so that he could keep them as souvenirs.

Sammy Tolliver was unusually subdued on his way up to Theatre, where Alex Marshall was waiting to pin his legs, but he managed a cheeky grin for Lauren on his way past, his little misshapen body seeming far too small on the enormous trolley.

His mother was walking along beside their son on his way to the lift, leaving Lauren standing by his father.

'She likes to go up with him while they give him the anaesthetic so I wait here, but I never get used to this—the waiting,' Mr Tolliver said to Lauren as he watched them go.

'That's because, although you've been through it so many times that you feel it should be old hat, logically you know that each operation carries the same chances for success and failure. And the bottom line is that Sammy's your son and you love him.'

A suspicious sheen of tears brightened the burly man's eyes and he had to clear his throat before he could speak.

'You've got it in a nutshell,' he confirmed gruffly, avoiding meeting her eyes as though embarrassed to show such emotions, especially in front of a younger woman. 'He's been through hell from the first moment he was born and yet he's such a...such a smashing kid.'

'Why not go up and tell him so?' she murmured quietly, her hand squeezing his arm for emphasis. 'There'll always be room for both of you to give him a hug and a kiss before he goes under the anaesthetic.'

He sniffed and wiped the edge of a surreptitious hand across the corner of one eye before he growled in an abashed tone, 'Thanks.' Then he hurried off to catch up with the trolley.

There had been no messages from Sunila by the time Lauren had finished assisting in Theatre so as soon as her duties were over she hurried across to the unit.

'Any news?' she demanded as soon as she saw Sunila, and her heart sank when she saw the expression on her face.

Before she'd opened her mouth to speak Lauren knew the news wasn't good.

'Someone's finally been in contact with the couple who were going to have Holly after she was born. You know, the couple who donated the eggs and sperm.'

Lauren nodded. 'And?'

'They got in touch with their solicitor who faxed the hospital's legal department. He informed them that as the two of them haven't been through any form of adoption, and as there isn't any proof that they bear any relationship to the child, it would be inappropriate for them to have any further involvement with said child.'

'Inappropriate!' Lauren exploded, moderating her voice with difficulty. 'We're talking about Holly's life here!'

'Hey! Don't kill the messenger!' Sunila said, the joking words at odds with her expression. 'I'm just as angry as you are. She deserves better than that.'

Lauren drew in a deep breath and held it while she fought for control.

'Sorry about that. Any news from the birth parents?'

'Not a word so far,' Sunila admitted. 'Noah said he

was thinking of getting the police to go round to see if the neighbours know where they've gone.'

'She's deteriorating, then?'

It had been a question but Lauren didn't really need an answer. She just had to look at the poor little scrap, fighting for every breath.

Lauren was suddenly aware that someone had come to stand behind her and, without turning to look, she knew that it was Jack. It wasn't just the fact that she recognised the scent of the soap he used or the elusive musk of his skin—it was almost like an electricity between them that hummed along every nerve.

'Poor little beggar,' he muttered, as the three of them stood, watching her. 'She's only got a slim chance and they won't even give her that.'

There was such depth of feeling in his voice that Lauren suddenly found herself wondering how he would have reacted to the death of their own child.

Had she made a mistake when she'd decided to cope with her pregnancy alone?

She knew he'd read her letter and had immediately gone away so she'd known that he hadn't been ready for a long-term commitment. But what would he have done if she'd actually managed to get in contact later, and had just asked for his emotional support until the baby was born?

Would it…could it have made a difference to the outcome?

As it was, not once in all the conversations… arguments…call them what you will… Not once had Jack mentioned their baby…

Suddenly the significance of that fact struck her like a ton of bricks and she nearly exclaimed aloud.

The last communication they'd had five years ago

had been her letter, telling him of her pregnancy. Nearly five years later they'd met up again, and while they'd nearly come to blows about the fact that he'd left her in the lurch neither of them had mentioned the fact that her child no longer existed.

The realisation was so startling that suddenly she needed to get away from him and do some hard thinking.

She needed to try to work out why a man who worked with children all day long and idolised his own son would completely ignore the existence of the child she'd been carrying.

The answer came to her like a flash of light in the darkness as she hurried along the corridor, and she had to lean against the wall as the consequences nearly blinded her with their brightness.

CHAPTER NINE

'DID Jack even read my letter?' Lauren said aloud, her voice echoing off the colourful walls of the empty corridor, the cartoon characters completely at odds with her thoughts.

One of the porters gave her a worried look as she stood there, muttering to herself, and she turned to make her way back to the ward with a blush on her face.

She'd intended to speak to her parents before she confronted Jack, but now it looked as if *all* her assumptions had been wrong.

What if—?

'No. Don't start that. Concentrate on the patients,' she murmured under her breath as she went to check each of them as they came up from the recovery room.

If she didn't leave herself time to think about the situation then the fact that she couldn't speak to Jack until they were both off duty wouldn't be quite so frustrating.

'Hello, Jilly,' she said softly, stroking the child's free hand to attract her attention.

'Mummy?' she mumbled, and opened her eyes to mere slits. She looked almost as if she were wearing a turban, with the bandage holding her ears in position wound around her head like that.

'No, darling, Mummy's here,' said the younger woman, sitting on the other side of the bed. 'I'm holding your hand, remember?'

The child's face lit up with a very sleepy grin.

'Doctor promised you'd be waiting for me,' she murmured happily.

'We're not going anywhere, Jilly,' her father added. 'Not till you're ready to come home.'

Lauren made a mental note to warn the two of them not to give in to the temptation to pamper their daughter *too* much and started to move on to the next bed.

When she realised it was Damien's bed she did a quick detour to Annie's office.

'Did that young nurse manage to get any photos of Damien?' she asked, when her friend came off the phone.

'Did she ever!' Annie exclaimed, as she reached into the drawer for a small stack of Polaroids. 'There's a couple of beauties!'

'A few of these would be very useful to keep around for future patients,' Lauren said, when she saw how much detail the instant photos had managed to show. 'It would be a lot easier to show them these, rather than trying to draw diagrams that look like a cross between a cat's cradle and a circus side-show.'

She chose the two that actually showed Damien's face as he'd slept his way through the whole thing and set off back across the ward.

'Hello, Damien,' she said, as she perched herself on the edge of the bed. 'Are you wide awake enough for a surprise?'

She was pleased to see that there was only his mother beside him, and hoped that his boisterous younger brothers would be kept away long enough to give him time to recover from the anaesthetic.

'A surprise?' he croaked, a small frown pleating his

forehead as he looked up at her. 'What sort of surprise?'

'Well, I thought it was very unfair that you wouldn't see any of your treatment so I asked the nurse who went up with you to take a couple of pictures.'

She spread them out in her hands so that he could see them.

'How does it feel to be a film star?' she teased.

'Oh, wow!' he breathed. 'Mum, look! It's me! And look at all that... It looks like...like an intergalactic ray gun!'

His mother was just as amazed as he was. Lauren watched her face fill with an awful fascination as she took in the sight of her unconscious son strapped to supports and suspended in a waterbath. The image intensifiers aimed at his kidneys *did* look very threatening.

'Oh, what a shame your father can't see these,' she said, not taking her eyes off the pictures.

'Paul and Simon will never believe it if they don't see the pictures,' Damien mourned. 'They said I wasn't having a proper operation if I wasn't having any stitches.'

'Well, in that case, perhaps you'd better keep the pictures,' Lauren suggested with a grin. 'You've got to have the proof if you're going to be able to make them jealous!'

'Oh, wow! Can I *really* keep them?'

'Really.'

'Thanks,' he said fervently, as he carefully took hold of them. 'Thank you very much.'

'Yes. Thank you, Doctor. You've been very good with him. I don't think I could have coped by myself.'

'You're welcome, but don't forget I've had plenty of practice,' Lauren pointed out. 'If I remember rightly, this is your first child to come into hospital for an operation. I have lots of children, coming in every day.'

'But that's not the way you treat them,' she said quietly. 'I can tell that you really care about each one, and it makes a difference.'

Lauren felt the wash of heat travel up her throat and knew that if she didn't escape quickly she would be caught blushing like a complete novice.

She said her farewells and continued around the rest of the ward, visiting everybody, while she checked up on all the post-operative patients.

In some cases they were already wide awake and wanting to talk, while others were still very woozy.

Kevin was a different child altogether. Not only did she have to scour the room to catch sight of him, but when she did she found him deep in an animated explanation of the complexities of computer warfare with another child.

'Yesterday he was so miserable that I felt guilty for leaving him here, even though I knew it was too soon after the operation. Today he looks as if he won't want to come home,' Kevin's mother said wryly.

'Well, who would have thought his problems were all because of a feather pillow?' Lauren countered. 'After an anaesthetic you hardly want to hear a child wheezing and fighting for breath. We were lucky it was something so simple and so easily curable.'

She left her to continue her conversation with the mother of the child in the next bed.

For the most part the atmosphere in the ward was so welcoming that parents were quite content to sit beside their offspring with the occasional foray to find a cup of coffee or chat to other parents.

That was one of the things Lauren liked about working in this department—the fact that the apparent air of informality was able to take a great deal of stress out of what could be a very stressful situation.

The last patient to return to the ward was Sammy Tolliver, after a total of eight hours in the operating theatre.

Lauren went over to spend some time with his parents, knowing that the severity of the operation meant that their son wouldn't be talking for some time.

'Dr Marshall spoke to us while Sammy was in the recovery room,' Mr Tolliver said, his wife's hand clutched firmly in his. 'He said he's very pleased with the way the operation went, and that once Sammy's over it he'll be able to start on physiotherapy to strengthen his muscles for walking.'

'I expect it'll make a big difference to him, being able to get himself in and out of his chair again,' Lauren said, smiling as she looked down at the wizened little body. It was hard to believe he was nearly eight years old when he wasn't as big as Danny at four.

'He's always been so fiercely independent that it's been very hard for him to have to get everyone to do everything for him,' his mother added, with a tearful smile. 'This will mean so much to him.'

'You can't help admiring his courage and the way he bounces back. He was telling me that he's already planning to have his arms done next. He's a very special little boy,' Lauren said, and meant every word.

The connection she'd made between Sammy and

Danny had her eyes straying to his bed on the other side of the ward.

She'd intended to save her visit to him until last so that she could spend some extra time with him. Unfortunately, his grandmother had arrived while she was busy, talking to Mrs Tolliver, and was sitting with him now.

Lauren hesitated.

There was no real need for her to see Danny at the moment—he'd developed no complications after the emergency operation and was recovering well. Except that she did enjoy her conversations with him, and had been looking forward to hearing his unique comments on life in general and life in a children's ward in particular.

However, with Jack's accusation about her treatment of his mother still ringing in her ears, she thought it might be better if she stayed away for the moment—at least until she could work out what she'd said to upset the woman. She could always see him after his grandmother had gone home.

The other patient weighing heavily on her mind was little Holly, and when she'd satisfied herself that there was nothing else she could do for her patients here she hurried across to the other side of the department.

As she pushed the door open she found herself reverting to the childish habit of crossing her fingers as she waited to find out what was happening.

'How is she?' she demanded as soon as she was close enough.

'Not good,' said Sunila, not bothering to sugar the pill. 'We're waiting for the police to get back to us.

Noah asked if they could see what they could find out about the surrogate parents.'

'How long ago was that?' Lauren glanced at the clock over the doorway.

'Several hours now, and she can't afford the time,' Sunila said bitterly. 'If we could only get them to sign the consent she could be on the table. That's all it would take.'

'Hey, Sunila, take it gently,' Lauren suggested quietly, worried when she saw the glitter of tears in the young staff nurse's eyes. She understood what the young woman was feeling because she, too, had been captivated by the tiny child's spirit, but working in this unit had quickly taught her the hard lesson that there weren't always happy endings. 'Even if the permission came back within the next couple of minutes you know it's no guarantee that she'll survive.'

Sunila drew in an audible breath and released it slowly as she reached for a tissue and blew her nose.

'I realise that,' she admitted honestly. 'I know some babies are operated on almost as soon as they're delivered, but it's really too soon for Holly. She needed several weeks of extra oxygen and special feeding so she could grow and build her strength up.'

'Or even months,' Lauren added. 'There's no doubt that she's too frail at the moment for the odds to be very good but, because she isn't responding well, to leave it any later isn't making things better—it's just lengthening the odds.'

'How soon will it reach the point where her chances of survival will be so bad that it won't be worth trying?'

'I don't know,' Lauren said honestly. 'I haven't had one go down so quickly before. I'm just glad that it'll be Noah's decision in the end. If it was up to me I'd want to give it a go on the basis that any chance is better than none.'

'Then you have to consider whether it's fair to put such a tiny baby through such horrendous trauma when there's so little chance that she'll survive,' Sunila said softly, the expression in her eyes more resigned now as she gently stroked Holly. 'Perhaps it's all for the best if we just make her last few days as comfortable as possible.'

All for the best. The phrase rang in Lauren's ears. That was what her parents had said when she'd finally returned home after she'd lost her precious baby.

'Perhaps it's all for the best, dear,' they'd said brightly. 'You're still young—only partway through your training. There'll be plenty of time to get married and have other children.'

Except that she hadn't *wanted* to have other children.

As time had passed she'd put her aversion down to grieving over the daughter she'd lost or to her increasing involvement in her career.

Even when their parents had taken advantage of the new closeness between Adrian and herself to push them into marriage it hadn't changed her mind.

She shuddered when she remembered the awful embarrassment of their wedding night when she'd discovered she couldn't bear to have him touch her with any sort of intimacy.

At the time they'd believed that the awkwardness had been because they'd been friends for so many years that they'd need time to see each other in any other role. Time had run out when Adrian had died, and Lauren had put all thoughts of marriage and children out of her head.

It wasn't until Jack had come to work at St Augustine's that everything had started to ferment in her mind. As she gazed sadly at Holly, fighting for breath, she finally realised that *he* was the answer to the questions.

Jack was the reason she hadn't been able to bear Adrian touching her. He might have deserted her when she'd needed him most and she might have believed that her love for him had died, but all she'd had to do was look at him and her heart had recognised the truth.

It was the same with babies.

Adrian had been only too willing to help her to have a child to replace the one she'd lost—by whatever means she was comfortable with—but she'd always found reasons to refuse.

It was seeing Jack with his son, Danny, that had finally made her realise that it was *Jack's* child she wanted to cradle in her arms... Only Jack's child would do.

It was with that thought still echoing inside her head that Lauren turned round and came face to face with the man in person.

'What's the matter?' she demanded, instantly knowing that something was very wrong. 'Jack, what's happened?'

'The police just got back to us,' he said, his voice coming out in the sort of jerky spurts that told Lauren he was having difficulty, controlling his anger.

'Apparently, they managed to speak to a neighbour of Holly's surrogate parents and, as far as he knows, the two of them have gone on holiday. He saw them putting suitcases in the car before they drove away.'

Lauren heard Sunila's gasp but she was too stunned to utter a sound.

'Can you believe it?' Jack demanded, his low voice more telling than a shout. 'Their daughter is lying in a hospital, fighting for her life, and they care so little that they can happily take a holiday!'

Lauren was horrified by the apparent callousness of the action, and part of her brain was racing at full speed, trying to come to grips with the situation.

'Could we have Holly made a ward of court so that we can go ahead and do the operation?' she suggested, and told him about a situation some while ago when a family had been involved in a car accident and none of them had been able to sign.

'I don't know whether this would come under the same heading as that,' Jack pointed out. 'It's not as if Holly's condition is the result of a sudden accident, and the courts could argue that, by going away, the parents have already tacitly stated their opposition to the operation.'

Sunila argued with Jack but the silent side of Lauren's brain had taken over so that she felt almost like an invisible observer.

This man, who was visibly furious that anyone could abandon a helpless child, was the same man that she had believed capable of reading a letter which told him that he'd fathered her child and then walking away from it without a word.

It was true that nearly five years had passed, and he'd obviously changed in the interim—Danny's very existence was proof of that. But had he really changed so much? Hadn't he *always* been this caring, concerned man?

'Anyway, it's worth a try,' Jack was saying, as Lauren focused on their conversation again.

As he walked away he was rubbing one hand over the back of his neck, as if the muscles in it had tightened up, and she wondered just how much real sleep he'd had since Danny had been rushed into hospital.

When she'd first known him she'd soon learned that if he fell asleep in a chair his neck tended to lock up, and her hands clenched as she fought the temptation to go after him and offer to ease it for him the way he'd taught her.

'In the meantime, she just has to keep fighting,' Sunila said sadly as Jack disappeared from view. 'The trouble is, we all know that her heart just isn't up to the job and it's going to reach a point...' She shook her head, knowing she didn't have to say the words.

'How are the rest of them?' Lauren said, deliberately turning her back on Holly and letting her eyes travel around the unit.

'Karl is definitely going to make it,' Sunila said with a genuine smile. 'Day is thrilled with him. His dependence on oxygen is already decreasing rapidly and, best of all, they've tracked down his family.'

'Fantastic!' Lauren exclaimed. 'Where are they—on holiday in London? Have they been to see him?'

'His father was in Germany but he's dropped everything and is on his way over as we speak. He was so pleased to hear from us that he was in tears.'

'Do we know what his wife was doing in London? He must be devastated to hear she'd died.'

'Apparently, she'd left him for another man before she realised she was pregnant and thought the new

bloke loved her so much that he wouldn't mind bringing up her child. When he finally walked out on her
because she wouldn't have an abortion—couldn't really because she was well beyond the legal limits—
she was stuck in London with no money.

'As far as the police can tell, she's been living
rough, and they think she hadn't eaten properly for
several weeks so she might just have gone light-
headed, keeled over and fallen into the road.'

'I'd rather think that than that she'd deliberately
tried to kill herself,' Lauren murmured, struck by the
messes some people made of their lives and how far
the ripples could spread.

'Leonie's been doing much better since we found
her a friend,' Sunila said, as she pointed to the surviving twin's cot.

'What is *that*?' Lauren exclaimed, when she saw
the peculiarly shapeless mass, sharing the cot with
their tiny patient.

'I think it's called a beanie or something,' Sunila
explained. 'It's a cloth toy filled with lentils. Anyway,
it was sterilised and put beside her as if it was her
twin and she's been much happier.'

'What do you mean—happier?' Lauren asked.

'Well, both her pulse and breathing have been far
more regular and she's far less restless.'

'Well, congratulations to whoever thought of that
one,' Lauren exclaimed in amazement. 'I certainly
wouldn't have.'

'Actually, it was Jack,' Sunila said. 'His son told
him about these toys—apparently, they've been very
popular with a certain age range.'

'Perhaps he needs to tell the manufacturer that the
age range has just been extended—' As she was

speaking the pager clipped to the top of her pocket began to bleep and she glanced at it quickly.

'Anything else needed here before I go?' she asked, her feet already taking her towards the door.

'No, nothing. Anyway, I can always page you,' Sunila said, and waved her off.

Lauren hurried out, wondering just what she was going to find when she reached the other end of the department. It wasn't too long ago that she'd visited each of the patients…except for Danny while he had his grandmother with him.

The problem was clear as soon as she pushed her way through the doors.

Poor little Sammy was coming out of the anaesthetic and was being horribly sick.

'All right, sweetheart,' Lauren crooned, as she swiftly administered another dose of the appropriate anti-emetic. 'That'll soon start working and then you'll stop being sick.'

'It hurts,' Sammy moaned, his misshapen arms wrapped around his stomach and his little face pale and sweaty. 'And my legs are so heavy I can't turn over to be sick.'

'Do you want us to turn you?' Lauren offered. 'Or would you rather do it yourself with just a little help?'

She was watching him fight his usual battle for independence when she felt the strange, tingling awareness that told her Jack was behind her.

'You can help,' Sammy agreed grudgingly, and as Lauren stepped forward he added, 'But be quick 'cos I'm going to…'

The rest of the words were lost in a bout of violent retching, and it was only Jack's lightning reactions that had the little chap gently raised and a bowl in position in time.

'Only just,' Sammy said weakly, when Jack laid him back down again. 'I hate making a mess.'

'In that case, let's get you organised in case you want to do that again before the new medicine works,' Jack said, and calmly set about organising Sammy's parents into rearranging his pillows and the casts on his legs until he was as comfortable as possible.

In the event, although Sammy said he felt sick, he didn't actually get as far as bringing anything up and was soon dozing peacefully while the anti-emetic and painkillers did their work.

'Poor little beggar,' Jack muttered a few minutes later as he scribbled on Sammy's notes. 'Whatever mixture they put in his drugs cocktail for the anaesthetic, something disagreed with him.'

'They'll have to check them against the ones he's had at previous operations and see if they can get it right next time,' Lauren said, as she watched him forming the bold, slashing outlines of his familiar handwriting. 'He's got enough to cope with without nausea.'

There was a brief silence between them as he finished writing and glanced around the ward. Then he looked at her with a slight frown between his eyebrows.

'I need to have a word with you where Danny can't hear us,' he said quietly as he slotted the paperwork away. 'Can we talk in Sister's office for a moment?'

'Of course.' She agreed instantly, wondering what had put that strange tone in his voice.

The door had barely closed behind them when he rounded on her.

'I just went to say goodnight to Danny and he's very upset. He said you didn't go to talk to him today,' he said accusingly. 'He said you talked to everyone else around the ward except him, and he wants to know if he's done something to upset you.'

'No!' she exclaimed, horrified that she might have hurt the little boy's feelings. 'Not at all. He's a lovely little boy and I enjoy spending time with him.'

'Then why didn't you speak to him?'

'Because...because your mother was sitting with him and I...I didn't want to intrude.'

He didn't say anything, but it was obvious from his expression that he didn't totally believe her.

'Well, last time I spoke to her you said I'd upset her,' she added defensively.

'Do you wonder at it when you threaten everything that she holds dear?' he countered sharply. 'Don't you think she's suffered enough for one lifetime?'

Lauren gazed up at him in amazement. What on earth was he talking about?

'I'm sorry, but I don't—'

'So you should be,' he grated. 'I kept my promise and now it looks as if you're trying to break yours. Well, let me tell you, if you think I'll let you get away with that you've got another think coming. Danny's my son and I love him but he means even more to her. When it looked as if she was going to die he was the one thing that made her keep fighting.'

'Wh-what?' Lauren gasped, the torrent of words coming at her too fast for comprehension. 'Your mother's been ill?'

'Oh, don't give me that!' he exclaimed in disgust. 'You know very well that she had cancer. I told you, that's why I had to go away.'

'Cancer?' she repeated. 'When did she have cancer? Where? She looks so well...' It was hard to imagine that the quietly elegant woman sitting beside Danny was having treatment for cancer.

'She's well now, thank goodness,' he stressed. 'But five years ago was a different matter.'

'Five years...?' Stricken, she looked up at him. 'Five years ago?' she said, as some of the missing pieces of the jigsaw finally slotted into place. 'Do you mean...? You left me to go to your mother?'

'I told you,' he said impatiently. 'She phoned me when she had the biopsy results and said she needed to go in for immediate surgery.'

'I never knew,' Lauren breathed, as her mind took her back to those awful days when she'd had no idea where he'd gone, no idea if she'd ever see him again.

'The first train only left me a few minutes to scribble the bare bones of an explanation, but I told you I'd tell you all about it when I got back...' He paused when he saw her shaking her head.

'I never got your note,' she said, as a terrible ache settled inside her.

If only she'd known why he'd gone... If only she'd known that he was coming back... If only...

'I came back to the flat that evening and it was in a mess. All I knew was that you'd grabbed a suitcase and some clothes and gone. I never heard from you again.'

'But I rang you several times from the hospital and left messages. That girl in the other flat on our floor took them, the one with the big...' He gestured with both hands cupped at chest level.

'Assets?' she supplied automatically, and suddenly realised that *that* had been the joke between them five years ago. 'The one who kept trying to kidnap you on the stairs?'

She'd almost forgotten about her. What was her name? Fifi, or Zuzu, or something. She'd been trying desperately to get into modelling or acting but with an eye out for a good-looking man at the same time.

Lauren had been worried at first, certain that she'd had so little to offer in comparison with such a worldly woman—and Jack was so handsome. It had been a source of great amazement to her that he hadn't even seemed to notice what the woman had been trying to do, and she'd delighted in teasing him about running the gauntlet each time he'd gone in and out of their flat.

'That's the one. She promised she'd pass on the messages to you and tell you the best times to ring back.'

Lauren closed her eyes and shook her head when she remembered how many times she'd asked... begged...the other woman to tell her if there had been any word from Jack.

'I never received any of them,' she whispered, never doubting for a moment that he'd tried to reach her.

The sound of several visitors, saying their good-byes, broke into the poignant moment and they both suddenly realised how much time had passed—both inside the room and since the disastrous events of five years ago.

'Have you got time to see Danny before you go home?' he said suddenly, a strangely vulnerable expression in his eyes.

Lauren wasn't certain whether he was asking because Danny wanted to see her or because their conversation had taken some of the heat out of his resentment. Perhaps it was a tacit way of offering her an olive branch?

Whatever the reason, she was only too willing to grasp it.

'Of course,' she said quickly, feeling the smile creeping over her face as she followed him out of the room. 'Your mother won't mind, will she?'

'She's not here,' he said, throwing the words back over one broad shoulder as he strode ahead of her. 'I took her to the station a little while ago to catch the train to London. She's staying the night with a friend before they spend the day shopping and gossiping and having their hair done. She'll be back late tomorrow afternoon when I take Danny home.'

'Hello, Danny,' she said softly as she reached his bedside. He was curled up on his side against a small Everest of pillows, smiling while he watched the Walt Disney video playing on the nearby television.

'Hello!' he said, his smile broadening into a happy grin when he saw who it was. 'I thought you'd gone home.'

'Not yet. I couldn't go home without coming to talk to you, now could I?'

She settled herself on the edge of the bed, and before she could stop herself she'd reached out a hand to smooth down his ruffled hair, loving the silky texture under her fingers.

Her glance flicked almost guiltily up to Jack's hair, so similar in appearance and feel, and collided with blue-grey eyes that hadn't missed a single thing.

'Daddy says I'm going home tomorrow,' Danny volunteered suddenly, then fell into a pensive silence before he continued in a rush. 'Will you come and see us at our house so I can talk to you?'

'Well, Danny,' she began, wondering how on earth she was going to tell him that she'd love to come and see him but there was the matter of his father's approval to seek.

'Daddy could bring you home with him and I could show you my secret place and you could read me a story when Granny's tired and you could help me to find just the right dog and—'

'Whoa, Danny, slow down,' Jack said, with a chuckle in his voice. 'One of these days I'll have to teach you about subtlety.'

'What's suttle-ty?' he said in all innocence.

'It's waiting for an answer to one question—like "would you like to visit our house?"—*before* you bury her under a host of other attractions.'

'Oh,' Danny said with a miniature frown, clearly unconvinced. 'Well, will you come?' he said directly, his heart in his eyes as he gazed up at her.

'I'd love to,' she said honestly, 'but—'

'But we'll have to sort out when it's convenient,' Jack added quickly. 'You only had your operation a little while ago so there's plenty of time.'

'No, there isn't, Daddy,' he whispered, grabbing his father's sleeve and tugging until he leaned closer—but still not close enough to stop Lauren hearing what he was saying. 'If I can only ask one question at a time 'cos of suttle-ty then I haven't got lots of time 'cos I like her and I want to ask her if she'd like to be my mummy.'

Lauren couldn't control the sudden gasp that escaped her, and she found herself pinned by two pairs of very intent eyes.

'Perhaps she doesn't want—' Jack began, but got no further because Danny had an agenda of his own.

'Have you got some children already?' he demanded, with the complete directness of young children.

'No, I haven't got any children,' she admitted quietly, the words hard in her throat so that she had to force them out. Then, to her horror, she found herself continuing, 'I had a baby once, but she died.'

'Oh,' Danny breathed, and one chubby hand appeared on top of her clenched fist. 'I'm sorry. Was she sick?'

'Yes,' Lauren whispered, as the sense of loss flooded through her again.

Lauren was so wrapped up in the twin emotions of grief for her loss and pleasure at Danny's innocent compassion that she almost didn't hear the sound of her pager.

'I'm sorry, Danny, but I've got to go,' she said with a slight sense of relief. Much more of that and she'd have been in tears in front of him. How could he have known that there was nothing she would have liked better than to have been his mother?

'Will I see you tomorrow?' he called as she hurried away.

'Before you go home,' she promised, then deliberately forced herself to think about the reason she'd been called to the other end of the department.

As she'd feared, Sunila beckoned her frantically as soon as she came through the doors.

'It sounds as if her lungs are filling up with fluid,' she said urgently. 'Can you do anything?'

Lauren's heart sank.

'I don't think we can. It sounds like secondary heart

failure and in that case…' She shook her head even as her eyes were scanning the read-outs and ECG traces on the various monitors.

A feeling of warmth stole over her from the back of her neck downwards, and she realised that Jack had joined them silently by Holly's cot.

'I don't think it's going to be very long now,' he murmured, his voice roughened by emotion. 'There's too little capacity left in her lungs to take in the oxygen she needs, and her poor heart can't pump the blood round fast enough to keep the oxygen going to her brain.'

A phone shrilled at the other end of the unit and was picked up almost immediately, but the three of them didn't move.

'Dr Madison?' murmured a voice, but Lauren didn't bother to turn. 'There's someone on an outside line who wants to speak to you. She says it's urgent.'

It was several minutes before Jack returned, several minutes in which she and Sunila watched as Holly visibly weakened, almost as if she'd finally given up the fight.

Lauren knew as soon as Jack came back to stand beside her because the air was almost vibrating with suppressed emotion.

'*That* was Holly's mother, phoning from Tenerife,' he said with venomous clarity in every syllable. 'She'd been thinking about it and feeling very guilty, and wondered if she should perhaps come in and sign the permission for the operation when they get back from their holiday.'

'Oh, God. Why didn't she think about doing it *before* she went away?' Sunila moaned softly, just as the heart monitor emitted a high-pitched warning that Holly's heart had finally stopped.

CHAPTER TEN

JACK guided his second-hand BMW between the imposing gate-posts and grimaced. It was chastening to realise that he still got an adolescent thrill out of the fact that he could afford such luxury now. When he'd first known Lauren he'd owned an elderly Mini, which had sounded more like a lawnmower, and could hardly afford the petrol to run it.

Even so, his first sight of Lauren's parents' home was enough to make his eyes widen. It wasn't a country estate, granted, but it was at least the size of a dower house. It looked as if it had been there for hundreds of years and was surrounded by immaculate gardens, just bursting into their full spring glory.

'No wonder they didn't want her involved with me,' he murmured with a twinge of understanding. Since he'd had Danny he could sympathise with parents, wanting the best for their child, and he'd be the first to admit that he wasn't exactly out of the top drawer.

As he circled the gravel drive to park he recognised Lauren's car and scowled. He'd hoped to get here before she did so that he could have this confrontation over, without hurting her, but...

He caught sight of the pieces of paper on the passenger seat and his resolve hardened.

It had been a terrible week since the evening Holly had died, and he'd longed to comfort Lauren in her silent grief but hadn't dared.

When he'd come face to face with her that first day at St Augustine's he'd wondered if he was going to be able to work with her.

It hadn't taken long before he'd discovered that his life wasn't nearly as satisfying as he'd thought. All he'd had to do was look at her and, in spite of the anger that had roared through him, he knew he still wanted her.

It had taken less than an hour, working with her, before he'd realised that she wasn't the uncaring person he'd thought she'd become, and from there it had been just a short step to wondering how many more of his conclusions about her had been drawn from misleading information.

He'd seen the sadness in her eyes when she'd told Danny about her daughter, and for the first time had realised that she'd wanted his child as much as *he* had.

For more than four years she'd mourned the baby she'd lost, and would probably mourn for ever unless…

Unless he confronted Lauren's parents with what he'd discovered. First he would have to force them to admit to their part. Only then would he be free to speak to her, to tell her that all the emotions he'd thought had died had only been sleeping.

Jack folded the papers and slipped them separately into the inner pockets of his jacket, refusing to let himself think about what she might say.

Over the last couple of weeks he'd caught her looking at him and thought he'd seen longing in her eyes. All he allowed himself to hope was that she regretted their parting even half as much as he did. In the end,

he'd decided that the only way to resolve everything
was to risk all on a single throw of the dice.

He'd overheard Lauren arranging to visit her parents for Mothering Sunday so he knew they would be
here. Now all he had to do was set everything in mo-
tion because his future happiness depended on it.

He drew a sharp breath and opened the car door,
slipping the keys into his pocket before he climbed
two shallow steps to the imposing front door and rang
the bell.

If he hadn't known that Lauren was an only child
he would have thought the woman who opened the
door was her sister. There was the same timeless
beauty to the structure of her face, and only when he
looked closer could he see the blurring of the edges
that gave away her age.

'Mrs Hamilton?' he said, calling on his years of
dealing with people in the most traumatic of situations
to keep his voice steady. No one had to know that the
hand hidden deep in his pocket was clenched around
his keys into a nervous fist. 'I wonder if I could have
a word with you and your husband about an important
legal matter?'

Lauren heard the bell ring as she sat on the end of
the bed in her old room and listened, hoping someone
else would answer the door. She wasn't ready to face
anyone else for a few minutes yet.

She glanced down at the papers clutched in her
hands and saw the way they were shaking, but what
she couldn't tell was whether the trembling was
caused by shock or anger.

She'd contacted Adrian's solicitor several days ago,
and when she'd explained that she was visiting her

parents for the day on Mothering Sunday he'd arranged to take the package waiting for her to his own home for her to collect.

Once it was in her hands she'd found that she'd wanted privacy to open it and had promised to contact him as soon as she could if the contents required any action.

She'd arrived home to find that her mother had taken advantage of her visit to invite several friends round for drinks.

The last thing Lauren had wanted was to stand and make polite conversation while Adrian's package was burning a hole in her bag. The realisation that several of the guests were suspiciously single young men had told her that her mother's agenda was unchanged. Before her mother could do anything about it, Lauren had made her excuses and disappeared up the stairs.

What she'd discovered when she'd opened the package had been enough to stop her heart.

She'd read each item and then reread them in growing disbelief, only peripherally aware that she heard the visitors leaving as she determined to confront her parents with what she'd learned.

Now there was another guest, and heaven only knew how long he would stay. She could tell it was a man because she could hear the deep voice in the hallway below.

Was he another of her mother's prospective sons-in-law? Had he been invited to share their meal with them? She certainly hoped not. With what she had on her mind, there was no way she would be able to make polite social chit-chat.

Moving quietly, she opened the door and stepped out just far enough to listen to the conversation going on downstairs. She should be able to tell if this was an invited guest or just a chance caller.

It was *Jack*, she realised as soon as she heard the voice clearly. What on earth was he doing here? And why today of all days?

Even as the thoughts were whirling round in her head her feet were taking her swiftly down the stairs.

'Oh, I think you're wrong,' he was saying, his voice reaching her clearly from the formal sitting room as she reached the hallway. 'I think the police would be *very* interested in the falsification of legal documents. Shall we phone them and find out?'

The mention of the police stopped her in her tracks. What on earth was going on between Jack and her parents?

'What I want to know is what you hope to gain by this,' her father said belligerently. 'We made an agreement and *we've* done nothing to break it. Are you telling me that after all this time you've changed your mind? No. I know what you're really after—money.'

'To have an agreement between two parties, both of them must know the facts of the situation,' Lauren heard Jack point out with steely control, totally ignoring her father's scurrilous accusation. 'If one of the parties—namely yourselves—has lied then there can be no agreement.'

'In which case, you'd have to prove it,' her father challenged, lofty disdain in his voice. 'Now, if you don't mind, we have invited a guest to share our meal and haven't got time for this nonsense.'

In the light of the papers she was clutching in her hand the arrogant condescension in his voice was the last straw. Suddenly she found herself striding across the last few feet before she appeared in the doorway.

'Oh, I'm sure our dinner won't spoil for the sake of a few minutes,' she said crisply, as she walked into the room. 'I, for one, would love to hear all about this agreement.'

'Lauren,' her mother gasped. 'We... I thought you were up in your room.'

'This is nothing you need to worry your head about,' her father said dismissively. 'Just a minor misunderstanding.'

'A minor misunderstanding,' she repeated slowly. 'I'm sorry but I'm afraid I don't see it that way.'

'How would you know?' he snapped. 'It's nothing to do with you.'

'Nothing to do with me?' she exploded, suddenly incandescent with rage as her hand clenched tightly around the proof that Adrian had left for her. 'You're talking about my child and you dare to say it's nothing to do with me.'

'Lauren,' her mother began placatingly, but only succeeded in drawing Lauren's attention.

'How could you *do* it?' she demanded. 'She was my daughter. How *dare* you lie and connive to steal her away from me? You had no right!'

'We did it for the best,' her mother said, her chin coming up as she armoured herself with her solid conviction. 'You were so young and you had a good future ahead of you—'

'She *was* my future!' Lauren interrupted furiously. 'She was my child and I loved her. What gave you the right to tell me that she'd died?'

She dragged in a sobbing breath, hanging onto her control by the merest thread.

'Do you have any idea how devastating that was—to wake up two days after she was born to be told she was gone? I never even saw her, never held her, never had a chance to tell her that I loved her.'

'Shh, Lauren, shh…' Jack soothed as he wrapped his arms around her and pulled her against his lean strength as he guided her to a nearby settee. One hand held a neatly pressed handkerchief and suddenly she realised that tears were streaming down her cheeks.

'Oh, Jack, I'm sorry,' she wailed as she burrowed against his shoulder. 'I didn't know what they'd done and now I'll never know where she is.'

'You've got no proof of any of this,' her father blustered stubbornly. 'Who's going to believe your ranting? They'll just put it down to delayed post-partum depression.'

'I don't think so,' Jack said quietly, the threat in his words all the more potent for his low voice. 'Especially when I can supply her with the proof.'

'Proof? What proof? There isn't any. You're just blowing hot air,' Mr Hamilton declared arrogantly, and strode across to sit in a huge throne-like chair.

'How about proof in the form of a notarised statement from Adrian?' Lauren challenged as she held up her hand to brandish the slightly crumpled documents. 'He was my friend and he cared about me, and when he saw how devastated I was about my baby's death he couldn't stand the guilt. That's partly why he took the overdose, but he made sure he left this for me by way of atonement.'

'It would never stand up in court,' her father declared. 'Half the county knew he spent most of his time out of his skull on drugs.'

'If he was that bad why were you so keen for me to marry him?' Lauren demanded hotly.

'Because at least he came from a decent family. He

wasn't some penniless upstart, dragging himself up out of the gutter by his bootstraps. This family has generations of achievement behind it. It's Adrian's credibility that would be questioned, not ours.'

'Poor Adrian was almost as much a victim as your daughter,' Jack pointed out icily, 'but I doubt whether even you could argue with the Registrar of Births, Deaths and Marriages.'

With a distinct lack of fanfare he withdrew a folded piece of paper from his pocket and handed it to Lauren, before wrapping his arm around her again.

With a last swipe at her tears she focused on opening the single sheet and reading it.

'I don't understand,' she said, as words and figures danced in front of her eyes. 'What is this?'

'Danny's birth certificate—or rather the forged certificate your father supplied when Danny was handed over to me,' Jack explained grimly. 'He probably thought he was being very clever and that no one would ever know what he'd done, but once I knew what I was looking for it only took five minutes to work it out.'

Lauren glanced from the certificate to her father but this time there was no glib disdain. Her mother, too, had abandoned her haughty stance and looked every day of her age as she moved like a sleep-walker to the chair closest to her husband.

'As far as I can find out, the doctor who attended you when you were in labour had been struck off the register until he got help for his drug addiction and was working illegally. That gave your parents the leverage over him to persuade him to tell you your baby had died.'

A mental image of the unsavoury little man's pale,

sweaty face told Lauren that Jack's assessment was probably correct. He had certainly seemed very nervous about something.

Jack turned from his explanation to fire his next comment directly at Lauren's parents.

'That's one thing about a pregnancy—it gives you plenty of time to do your planning. Unfortunately for you, it also gave me time to come looking for Lauren.'

'You were looking for me?' Lauren said, and the cold bands around her heart loosened a little more.

'What do you think?' he said, and as he looked down at her she saw the once-familiar glint of light in his stormy grey-blue eyes. 'I was worried about you when you just disappeared like that without a word. I needed to know that you were all right.'

'And that's how you found out about the baby,' she said, glad that one of her questions had now been answered.

'Only because your father lost his temper and let it slip,' Jack pointed out. 'Then, when I said I was coming to get you, to take care of you during the pregnancy, he said not to bother. You were going to have an abortion.'

'No!' Everything in her revolted at the idea of killing Jack's baby. She'd never contemplated it for a moment, not even when she'd thought Jack had abandoned her.

'That's when he persuaded me that if I would stay away from you he would try to influence you to let the baby live. If I agreed he would hand the baby over to me when it was born.'

'But…' The plan was so monstrous that she couldn't help staring at her parents in disbelief.

Her mother at least had the grace to look guilty, but her father's mouth had tightened into its all-too-familiar self-righteous sneer.

'Then they realised that they were going to have to register the baby's birth because they knew I was going to need a certificate. It must have come as a nasty shock to find that you either need a marriage certificate to register a baby in the names of both father and mother or, if they're unmarried, the father and mother both have to attend in person.'

'Otherwise...?' Lauren wasn't quite sure where the explanation was going.

'Otherwise the father's name won't be on the certificate and he'd have to apply to the courts to adopt.'

'And that's when you would have contacted me for my permission and found out that my baby was supposed to be dead.'

'And they couldn't risk that,' he agreed, focusing on her as he spoke as though there were just the two of them in the room.

'So how did they get the registrar to put all the details on this certificate?' Lauren wanted to know as she scanned it again.

'I can only guess that, as you were to know nothing about it, your mother must have registered the baby, using your birth certificate. She'd never have got away with it if she hadn't looked so young.'

'But your name is on here too, and you said you would have to go to the registrar with her for that to happen.'

'So I would—if this was a genuine copy of the entry in the register,' he pointed out, as he reached into his pocket again and drew out another folded sheet of paper. 'Whereas, if you look at the copy I obtained on Thursday you'll see that there is no mention of the father's name.'

'But... How could they do that?'

'I've a feeling that's what the police are going to want to know, but at a guess it involves a special solvent to remove the permanent ink and some rehearsal to perfect a matching style of handwriting to fill in the missing details of the child's father.'

Lauren didn't bother to look at her parents for confirmation. She was far too busy, comparing the two certificates.

'But the only difference between the two is that your name has been filled in the space for the father,' she pointed out. 'How did they persuade the registrar to change the sex from female to male?'

'They didn't, Lauren,' he said gently, cupping her chin to bring her face up so that their eyes met. 'That was just another one of your parents' lies. Your baby didn't die and it wasn't a girl.'

'Then...?' Her eyes brimmed with tears as all the pieces of the jigsaw seemed to fall into place. She was almost too afraid to hope.

'Yes.' He nodded. 'Danny is your son...*our* son.'

'Happy Mother's Day,' Jack said as he made room on the bedside cabinet for two cups of tea and swooped to brush a fleeting kiss across her lips.

'Is there room for another one there?' he asked as he scooped up a cat with each hand and deposited them on the floor.

Desperate Dan glared at him balefully before he stuck his tail up in the air and stalked out of the room, closely followed by Jack the Ripper.

'I don't really like them coming on the bed, but they seem to be fascinated by this little one.'

Lauren stroked a gentle finger over the cap of dark silky down covering the baby's head, then bent to deposit a kiss.

'Has she finished her feed?' Jack asked as he reached eager hands out for her.

'Full to bursting and fast asleep,' Lauren reported, smiling when she saw the familiar besotted expression on his face as he gazed down at his tiny daughter.

'Those cats aren't the only ones fascinated by her,' he murmured, as he wandered over to the window to look out at the garden, drawn by the sound of excited laughter.

Lauren joined him, wrapping her arms around his waist and leaning her head on his shoulder as she shared his bird's eye view of Danny.

'At the moment he's far more excited about the puppy,' she said wryly, as she watched the two of them, racing round in a frantic game of tag.

A flash of pale orange in the shrubbery caught her eye, marking the amateur stalking progress of the other new addition to the family.

'A new baby, a new puppy *and* a new cat all in the same month—we must be mad.'

'Ah, but what a glorious madness,' he murmured as he put his other arm around her. 'Who would have thought, just one year ago, that things would turn out this way?'

Lauren felt her smile dim a little when she remembered that awful confrontation with her parents and the endless hours of interviews and statements that had followed.

The only good thing about it was the fact that she

and Jack had realised that they had both been victims of others' selfishness, and with all guilt wiped away they'd been able to regain the happiness they'd shared before.

Even her parents had finally realised that the best person for their daughter was the man she loved. They would never be particularly close, but were slowly discovering the unique joys of becoming grandparents.

She tightened her arm around him and gave thanks for the serendipity that had brought Jack to St Augustine's.

'I certainly didn't think we'd be standing here in our own home—'

'The home you and Danny persuaded me to buy just because it had a secret seat in a little boy's bedroom,' he interrupted.

'And because there are wonderful trees in the garden, and views of open countryside right to the horizon, and plenty of room for children and dogs to run and play, and—'

'And plenty of room for my mother to know that she's always welcome, even though she's just discovered a hidden wanderlust. And, most of all, a lovely big bedroom just for the two of us, with a door to separate us from the rest of the world,' he continued, with a sly glance in her direction.

'Do you think that Jane is ready to be put to bed?' Lauren suggested, feeling the familiar warmth begin to invade her limbs in direct response to the expression in Jack's eyes.

'I'm hoping that Jane's *mother* is ready to be put to bed,' he countered wickedly. 'Danny's in seventh heaven out in the garden and your parents aren't due to join us until this evening so, with any luck, that will give us enough time to discuss the various aspects of Mothering Sunday.'

'Discuss?' she repeated with a chuckle, her heart overflowing with the happiness she'd found with him as she watched him settle Jane into her cot with loving care. 'That's a new word for it!'

'Well, every discussion has to start off by using mouths to open the conversation, and some people find they can't talk properly unless they're using their hands as well...'

Silence fell as he began to demonstrate the concept, and she'd just reached the point where the outside world began to fade away when there was the sound of rapid footsteps pounding up the stairs.

'Mummy! Daddy! Calamity's stuck in the tree!'

They just had time to make themselves presentable before Danny flung open the door and raced in.

'You've got to come and help her. She can't get down,' he exclaimed, as he hopped from one foot to the other.

The year had made a big difference to him, too, Lauren thought fondly, seeing how long and coltish his legs had grown and how much older he seemed since he'd taken on the serious responsibilities of being an older brother.

'Danny, how many cat skeletons have you seen dangling in trees?' Jack asked, the husky tone in his voice telling Lauren that he wasn't nearly as cool and calm as he sounded.

'Well, none,' he admitted.

'Doesn't that tell you that cats are perfectly well able to get down out of a tree if they've climbed up in it in the first place?'

'But she's Calamity Jane,' he exclaimed, giving their most recent addition to the family her full name. He'd insisted that as he and his father both had a cat named after them the new baby should too.

Unfortunately, the first part of her name wasn't accidental. If a cat could get into trouble *she* would.

'All right,' Jack conceded, throwing Lauren a long-suffering look. 'Go and tell her I'm on my way.'

Danny shouted his agreement as he raced out of the room and thundered his way back down the stairs.

'I suppose this means that we're going to have to wait for our private celebration of Mothering Sunday until everyone's gone to sleep tonight,' he grumbled, as he straightened his clothes.

'Unfortunately, that's part of what Mothering Sunday's all about,' Lauren pointed out, having a hard time hiding her grin.

'Well, all I can say is I'm looking forward to Father's Day,' he said. 'Have you ever noticed that although it comes three months after Mother's Day it's also significant that it comes nine months *before* it.'

He started to walk out of the bedroom as Lauren fired her parting shot.

'When we start our "discussion" this evening you'll have to tell me whether you meant that as a threat or a promise…'

MILLS & BOON®

Makes
any time
special

Enjoy a romantic novel from
Mills & Boon®

Presents™ Enchanted™ Temptation.

Historical Romance™ Medical Romance™

MILLS & BOON®

Medical Romance™

COMING NEXT MONTH

AN UNEXPECTED BONUS by Caroline Anderson
Bundles of Joy

Dr Ed Latimer had said he couldn't have children, but Jo was quite definitely pregnant! It was a wonderfully unexpected bonus, but Ed's reaction wasn't quite what Jo expected.

THE LOCUM AT LARCHWOOD by Janet Ferguson

Dr Kate Burnett and the locum, Guy, were beginning more than a working relationship—until her ex-boyfriend came back...

UNDO THE PAST by Gill Sanderson

Senior Registrar John Hawke could see Lauren was holding people at bay, but if he could persuade her to make him part of her life, maybe he could solve the problem.

AN UNGUARDED MOMENT by Helen Shelton

Dr Ginny Reid was shocked when her practice partner and best friend, Mark, wanted to leave. He'd been patient long enough, waiting for Ginny to understand her feelings...

Available from 2nd April 1999

Available at most branches of WH Smith, Tesco, Asda, Martins, Borders, Easons, Volume One/James Thin and most good paperback bookshops

MILLS & BOON®

A man for mum!

Mills & Boon® makes Mother's Day
special by bringing you three new
full-length novels by three of our
most popular Mills & Boon authors:

Penny Jordan
Leigh Michaels
Vicki Lewis Thompson

On Sale 22nd January 1999

FREE

2 BOOKS
AND A SURPRISE GIFT!

We would like to take this opportunity to thank you for reading this Mills & Boon® book by offering you the chance to take TWO more specially selected titles from the Medical Romance™ series absolutely FREE! We're also making this offer to introduce you to the benefits of the Reader Service™—

- ★ FREE home delivery
- ★ FREE monthly Newsletter
- ★ FREE gifts and competitions
- ★ Exclusive Reader Service discounts
- ★ Books available before they're in the shops

Accepting these FREE books and gift places you under no obligation to buy; you may cancel at any time, even after receiving your free shipment. Simply complete your details below and return the entire page to the address below. **You don't even need a stamp!**

YES! Please send me 2 free Medical Romance books and a surprise gift. I understand that unless you hear from me, I will receive 4 superb new titles every month for just £2.40 each, postage and packing free. I am under no obligation to purchase any books and may cancel my subscription at any time. The free books and gift will be mine to keep in any case.

M9EC

Ms/Mrs/Miss/Mr ....Initials ....
BLOCK CAPITALS PLEASE

Surname...

Address..

....

....Postcode ....

Send this whole page to:
THE READER SERVICE, FREEPOST CN81, CROYDON, CR9 3WZ
(Eire readers please send coupon to: P.O. Box 4546, DUBLIN 24.)

Offer valid in UK and Eire only and not available to current Reader Service subscribers to this series. We reserve the right to refuse an application and applicants must be aged 18 years or over. Only one application per household. Terms and prices subject to change without notice. Offer expires 30th September 1999. As a result of this application, you may receive further offers from Harlequin Mills & Boon and other carefully selected companies. If you would prefer not to share in this opportunity please write to The Data Manager at the address above.

Mills & Boon is a registered trademark owned by Harlequin Mills & Boon Limited.
Medical Romance is being used as a trademark.

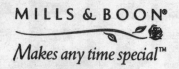

MILLS & BOON®

Makes any time special™

The Regency Collection

Mills & Boon® is delighted to bring back, for a limited period, 12 of our favourite Regency Romances for you to enjoy.

These special books will be available for you to collect each month from May, and with two full-length Historical Romance™ novels in each volume they are great value at only £4.99.

Volume One available from 7th May